THE EGO'S
NEST

THE EGO'S NEST

DAVID CHARTERS

E&T

First published 2011 by Elliott and Thompson Limited
27 John Street, London WC1N 2BX
www.eandtbooks.com

ISBN: 978-1-9076-4223-4

9 8 7 6 5 4 3 2 1

A CIP catalogue record for this book is available from
the British Library.

Printed and bound in the UK by CPI Cox & Wyman

For unreasonable men and women everywhere.

Author's note

HE HAD to come back. Why is it that bad people are so resilient? And, I suppose he had to try to get the girl. Not just any girl, but The Girl. As investment bankers go, Dave Hart is now operating not at the 30,000 feet altitude of the senior manager, but at 90,000 feet, as only he can. Helping me get him there have been a number of people, who made suggestions, read and re-read, and gave me thoughts and ideas, and I remain grateful to them as ever. In particular, Adam Shutkever, Joanna Rice, my son Mark and daughter Anna, and of course Jane, all deserve special mention, as well as Lorne, Olivia and the team at Elliott and Thompson. And for the inspiration for Dave Hart, my thanks to the men and women who work in the Square Mile and the West End, in particular my friends in the hedge fund industry.

David Charters

London

May 2011

I'M ABOUT to blow up a cow.

Not an inflatable one. My lips will not be involved. A real one. An actual bovine monstrosity.

It's standing quietly, chewing moronically on some grass, about thirty yards in front of me. It's vaguely off-white, not the clean Friesian black-and-white I'm used to in England, and it's tethered to a wooden stake.

I'm crouching behind a fence, preparing to fire an ex-Soviet rocket-propelled grenade launcher – an RPG-7 – that is going to convert my vegetarian friend into lumps of red meat.

Why am I doing this? Because I can. I've never done it before and I'm told it's interesting. I've done everything else. Well, everything you can do unless you're the president of the United States. I haven't declared global thermonuclear war. Not yet, anyway.

So here I am, a former investment banker who made out like a bandit – arguably was a bandit – but who escaped before the full awfulness of the crash and squirreled away his haul, his billions, in a mega scam before the music stopped.

I was short. And I don't mean physically challenged (although I am). Indirectly, I'd sold the shares not only of my own company, which I was steering resolutely on to

1

the rocks, but also of every other firm. I knew the whole industry would be caught out when the world finally woke up and realised that investment bankers were indeed naked emperors, wandering around in the ultimate glass house, their firms trapped in a cycle of inter-dependency that meant when one went down, they all would. And I was certainly going to make sure that mine did.

I was running the Erste Frankfurter Grossbank, the biggest bank in the world (at least by some measures), and with remarkable prescience I saw the crash coming and, with some well-placed co-conspirators, made my plans. We were short when it made sense to be, placed our bets ahead of the crowd – big bets – and my friends profited handsomely.

And so did I. Privately. And Grossbank was brought to its knees by its own management. By me. And then the whole pack of cards came down.

All those trillions that were pumped into the system by the world's central banks had to go somewhere, didn't they? For every trade in the market there are two sides, a buyer and a seller – or, in this case, a winner and a loser. I was the winner.

None of it was public. I was chairman of Grossbank, a pivotal figure for the biggest player in the market, and of course, my actions were always in the interests of shareholders, employees, customers, market counterparties, regulatory authorities and all of our other stakeholders.

Yeah, right. When the banking sector collapsed and share prices fell through the floor, the smart money made billions.

I like billions.

The cow turns its head and looks in my direction. It's a Cambodian cow. That's where I've been since faking my death – a melodramatic simulated death plunge from Blackfriars Bridge onto the heavily-cushioned deck of a barge owned by an associate of mine.

So now I'm a dead man. Officially. Now I have a new name. I'm no longer Dave Hart. Pity. I liked Dave Hart, was kind of used to it. But now I'm someone else. And I'm here in Cambodia, discreetly enjoying whatever pleasures remain to the jaded, saturated, cynical, worn-out ex-investment banker who's finally come to the end of his road.

This is what the Cambodians allow super-rich hedge fund managers, private-equity gurus, investment bankers and other grotesquely wealthy, time-sensitive, adrenalin junkies to do to their livestock for what they think is a lot of money. Stupid? Of course they are. But it's amazing what poor people will sell for the wrong price. Speaking as a rich person, I have no problem with that.

I squeeze the trigger.

'*Th . . . whoooop!*'

A brief kick in my shoulder and out it goes. The ex-Vietcong instructor gives me a supportive pat on the back as the projectile flies high in the air, missing the cow by about ten yards. I wish I could have tethered some of my old colleagues from Grossbank there but obviously that's not practical, though it might have improved my aim. We wait, and after a few seconds the grenade explodes somewhere vaguely in the distance. I hope it didn't hit a village.

Big loss of face. Or not. I'm paying the fees, after all. My instructor shouts at the black-pyjama clad team members who have appeared from nowhere and are untethering the cow to bring it ten yards closer. Whatever happened – or didn't – was clearly their fault. He berates them appropriately and nods at me encouragingly. It's just a matter of time.

They reload me and I stare down the sights a second time. The cow fills them completely. I can see nothing other than the cow. I know I'm an investment banker, but surely even I can't miss?

'Th . . . *whoooop!*'

Gotcha! Awesome. A huge thump, followed by a flash and a bang, and lumps of meat are flying through the air.

Thought you could defy me, you fucking bovine loser? Think again. You are Lehman Brothers in my sights.

Then something wet thwacks me in the face, something clingy and unpleasant. Something that bursts my bubble . . .

I'M AWAKE.

My eyes open and I stare at the fan on the ceiling. I'm lying on a monster-sized semicircular bed that is covered with beautiful, naked Cambodian women with long, dark hair that reaches almost to their waists, their bodies still glistening with the oils they rubbed into each other and then into me. Full body massage by numbers. Why choose when you can have them all? I count six, seven, eight of them, all stunning, lithe and, most of all, available. They are snoozing, or pretending to, after the exertions of last night. Or, at least, the pretend exertions. I didn't make much effort myself, just took in the show and let them do their stuff.

There are guys who call them LBFMs – Little Brown Fucking Machines. I hate that term. For one thing it's inaccurate. These girls suck as well. Boy, do they suck. And they have wonderfully delicate hands, and some of them have an amazingly firm grip. And the best part of all is the well-oiled body-to-body massage. I'm no misogynist. I love women. All of them.

Or I used to.

I glance down at an empty bottle of champagne in an ice bucket. The ice has long since melted. There's an ashtray next to it with a couple of cigar stubs and a lot of ash. The detritus that remains from another great time. Yeah, right. I'm getting bored with all these good times.

There was a moment last night when one of the girls was kneeling at my feet, about to go down on me, staring up at me with her huge, dark eyes, and she asked if I was ready. Ready? Me? Is the Pope a Catholic? But, then it struck me, just how unexcited I actually was at the prospect of yet another technically perfect, brilliantly executed professional blow job that meant absolutely nothing and would be forgotten the next day.

The problem with meaningless, empty sex is that it's so meaningless and empty. Better a well-intentioned amateur who puts her heart into it than the most technically perfect professional who really doesn't care.

When a man tires of blow jobs he tires of life. Surely a man in his forties can't tire of life? I should have decades of blow jobs ahead of me. Am I having a nightmare? Is that what my future holds? Desperately searching the globe for something stimulating to do, because I've ticked all the pleasure boxes I know and I can't live without the possibility of something new?

The problem is I have to remain hidden. I committed the perfect crime, a crime which no one knows has been committed and, anyway, they all think I'm dead. Ask the average banker if he'd turn his back on his life and disappear forever, given a few billion to cushion the blow, and he'd say yes in a heartbeat. I did. But now I'm more than nine months into my new life of anonymous super-wealth and I'm already regretting it.

The point about success is that you enjoy it principally through the eyes of others. People who spend their lives in the jungle of the City are fundamentally empty on the inside. I know I was. I believed in nothing, wanted everything, and my goal was to have more and more. Of everything. Money, power, possessions, booze, drugs and, of course, pussy. But I wanted most of it, not for the rush it gave me, which was only ever temporary, but because others didn't have it. Or, if they did, I got there first and had more than they did. And that's why I came up with the greatest scam of all time.

And it worked.

It worked because a few of us, myself on the inside and my two co-conspirators on the outside, brought down the global financial system. It needed an insider. I was that insider. I drove Grossbank onto the rocks and, in the process, blew the whistle on the rest of the major investment banks. I called time. But only when I was ready and my friends were ready too.

Rom Romanov was the big financial muscle, awesomely connected in a London-Russian-global-Jewish kind of way. Hugely wealthy, a man of a certain age who appears totally ageless, dark-haired, fresh-faced, apparently woken from whatever cryogenic chamber the undead are kept in. He even has a clammy handshake. But there are worse sins. At least from the undead.

Bang Bang Lee is easier. He's a classic Chinese tycoon, known for his propensity for offering competitors two lead injections in the back of the head, which makes even the most difficult counterparties review their position. It's amazing how often people see sense once they have the time to reflect.

So Rom and Bang Bang are friends and collaborators. And billionaires – even before the crash. Now they won't have enough fingers and toes to count their billions.

They brought a lot of other people in too – friends of theirs, Chinese tycoons, Russian oligarchs, Mafia dons and cartel chieftains. The villains had a good crash.

Some people would feel uncomfortable about that. Not me. Markets are morally neutral swings and roundabouts. And as an investment banker, I really don't care who the winners and losers are, as long as I get my cut. And I certainly did – the biggest ticket of my life.

Which makes it strange that I really don't feel happy. Or proud. Or even satisfied. They say it's better to travel than to arrive. But what if you arrive and nobody notices? Something's missing. No. Someone's missing. The only person who could really touch me.

Two Livers.

The woman I'm thinking of is unique. Yes, yes, they're all unique, but this one really is. Laura 'Two Livers' MacKay – the smartest woman in the City of London – named for her massive capacity for consuming alcoholic drinks of every kind while remaining not just bright, sober and charming, but utterly, timelessly, breathtakingly beautiful. An intelligent blonde who could melt my heart.

While I was sailing away into history, she was round at the Bank of England, desperately trying to save the firm. Someone had to.

Christ, how I miss her.

I'M IN a cage underwater, attached to the back of a large motor cruiser, breathing off a regulator which is attached to a compressor on the boat, staring out into the deep blue waters of the Pacific. The boat itself is superbly luxurious. I could afford to buy half-a-dozen and not even notice, but I'm following the golden rule of wealth preservation: if it floats, fucks or flies, rent it. Beside me, an instructor shares the cramped space in the cage, scanning the ocean around us.

We have full face masks and a radio that allows us to talk.

He's shaking his head. 'I'm sorry, this has never happened before. That huge one seems to have disappeared.'

The giant he's talking about is a great white shark, all of four metres long and with the kind of cold, killer eyes that I never saw on the trading floor. At least not at my firm. I heard that the US firms might have been different.

Anyway, we'd been circling in the boat for the two hours, searching the sea for fins, dragging lumps of tuna on lines behind the boat and tipping buckets of blood into the water. Finally our patience was rewarded, not just with fins, but with an explosion of activity as the bait was taken. The lines were severed by rows of razor-sharp teeth and a huge predator cruised past, its head breaking the surface as it seemed to stare up at us, weighing us up as its next potential meal.

Another day, another adrenalin rush. Cage diving with a great white shark. It's there so it had to be done.

I'd shaken off the topless blonde Ukrainian who was massaging suntan oil into my shoulders. I'm wearing tiny Speedo budgie smugglers and she'd offered to cream me up everywhere if I was willing to do the same for her. What could I say? I'm a guy. Don't expect depth. But she'd still be there later, so I headed below with my instructor and kitted up in double-quick time, climbed into the cage and we were lowered to the optimal viewing depth.

Which is when nothing happened. As soon as I entered the water, the shark circled once, having a look at us, then took off. The crew kept throwing in buckets of blood and dangled more lumps of tuna next to the cage, but it was hopeless. So they keep us down there for another twenty minutes because it's possible the shark was spooked by an even bigger shark – the only thing that scares a great white is an even bigger great white – and there had been reports in the area of a monster up to six metres long.

But if there's a monster around, I figure it has to be the one in the cage.

The instructor turns to me and points to the surface with his thumb. I nod and they raise the cage and release us.

When we're back on board they all look uncomfortable. They say that they have never seen them behave that way before. Its fins broke the surface, heading fast away from us, as if all it wanted was to get out of Dodge.

There isn't much I can say, so I crack a few jokes about ex-bankers and professional respect, but privately I see it differently.

Living this life has made me toxic, even underwater.

I WISH I was at Duke's – the hotel in St James's Place. Or, more specifically, the bar where Alessandro – London's finest barman – produces the best dry martinis on the planet. And I only drink Uluvka, the world's best premium vodka. When it comes to indulging myself, I like to think I'm not only knowledgeable, focussed and determined, but utterly uncompromising. If self-indulgence were an Olympic sport, I'd be a gold medallist.

The act of preparing a martini is an art in itself. A sort of hushed reverence surrounds the ritual by which pre-chilled glasses are anointed with the tiniest hint of vermouth before frozen vodka is poured in and a twist of fresh lemon added, in a precise, unhurried process that defies the pressures of the twenty-first century.

No matter how much I try – and I have, in countless places all around the Pacific Basin – no one has come close to matching London's finest. Which is irritating, because being super-rich is supposed to mean I get to have it all. And the thought of never going back there again is intolerable. What are my billions for if I can't get a decent martini?

On the other hand, being dead has its lighter side.

The best bit was the obituaries. I'd never really thought before about the process by which lives are assessed, summarised, put on paper and preserved for all time. Real life is full of ambiguities, half truths, accidents and happenstance. Life in the obits is linear, deliberate and one dimensional, with only the occasional allusion to the multiple shades of grey that make the real thing infinitely more interesting than the 2,500 words squeezed between a World War Two fighter ace and a long-retired chief government scientist.

I could detect the hand of Ball Taittinger, my ace public-affairs advisers, and specifically the Silver Fox, their sixty-something, seen-it-all, smooth and charming chairman – at least in the friendlier ones: '. . . the greatest banker of them all, a man who built the biggest firm in the world only to see it crash before his eyes as the result of market forces beyond his control. But unlike lesser men, he took responsibility for what he felt was a failure of leadership, and he paid the ultimate price.'

I read these sitting in the sun on a beach with perfect white sand in Thailand, the sound of the ocean gently lapping against the shore in the background. I had the whole place to myself, except for the beautiful Thai girl whose head was bobbing up and down in my lap while I flicked through the papers. Dead? Moi? You must be kidding.

All the obits mentioned the fact that my body has never been found. Of course it hasn't been found. I still have it. It's where I live. But they don't know that, and it adds a touch of mystery and glamour.

But some of the other remarks were less flattering. 'He lived life to the full' was probably the most euphemistic, penned, I suspect, by the Silver Fox or one of his team, in sharp contrast to others. 'He was a notorious womaniser and bon viveur, frequently under the influence of drugs and alcohol, even while at work, and determined to push the boundaries of excess to the limit.' Well, yes, but what are boundaries for? And are you jealous, or what?

Another mentioned the succession of lawsuits from female employees claiming sexual harassment that plagued me at Grossbank. As if history will give a damn about whines from the little people who won't even merit a footnote.

Yet another described me as having a naturally addictive personality. Well, yes, I'm addicted to pleasure. Isn't everyone? It's just that some of us do something about it.

I felt a strange detachment from the things I read, as if they were written about someone else, which, in a sense, they were. But the memorial service was different.

The memorial service was held at St Lawrence Jewry, the official church of the Corporation of London. Three hundred people attended. Three hundred! If you want a packed church, die young. The whole of the City establishment was there, presumably because for one hour, starting at eleven o'clock that Thursday morning, it was the place to be and to be seen. The greatest irony was that, like almost everyone there, I was – and still am – an atheist, but that minor detail shouldn't get in the way of a good show.

The reality in twenty-first century Britain is that money is the one true god. We all defer to it, and I suppose people realised I had a lot of it, so deserved respect. They had no idea quite how much.

Looking at photos of those who attended, the people I worked with for years, my friends, my comrades in arms, I felt . . . nothing. I recognised people whose fortunes I had made with my decisions in the annual bonus round, with a move to Hong Kong or New York, a promotion, the authorisation for a particularly risky trade. And there were others there whom I had destroyed with a signature on a piece of paper or a click of my mouse to send an email. Sometimes they were the same people, with only an alarmingly short time between the two moments. It rarely had much to do with talent or hard work, or even that most fickle of mistresses in the Square Mile, actual success. When you play in the high-stakes room in the casino, you don't complain when you win, and you shouldn't when you lose, however random, arbitrary and utterly unfair it all seems.

And then there was my 'family', that is to say my ex-wife, Wendy, and Samantha, the daughter I never bothered to know, but for whom I cleaned out Hamleys and the toy department at Harrods on countless occasions. She's almost seven now, and what amazes me most of all is my complete absence of curiosity about her. She's a stranger and I see no reason to change that. Does that make me a monster? Or just a realist? All I see is another appalling Chelsea teenager in the making, yah-yahing her way along the King's Road, wearing the same awful skinny jeans, Ugg boots and hoodie and spending her time building up to the amazing moment when Rupert or Rodney, a handsome but vacuous, well bred but inbred twenty-three-year-old estate agent, who served in the Guards or the Cavalry, will ask her to be his bride: 'Daddy, I've got wonderful news! I'm engaged. Rodney asked me to marry him!' Yippee, squeal, jump up and down, put the hand out for the wedding, the honeymoon, the starter apartment near Sloane Square, the little BMW to run around town in, and eventually the private room in the Lindo Wing at St Mary's Paddington as the babies pop out and then the school fees fund, and the whole self-perpetuating charade grinds on. Why can't I get excited about it the way other fathers do? They do, don't they? They always say they do.

I've learnt that Wendy has engaged some expensive probate lawyers to fight about my estate. She had a shock when she learnt about my will. Apparently, she doesn't see the funny side of my leaving everything to the Battersea Dogs' Home and thinks she should have it instead – for Samantha's sake, of course.

There was one heart-rending moment, just one, when I flicked open *The Times* and saw a photo of Two Livers, radiant in a black dress – it looked like silk, by Chanel – with a matching black wide-brimmed hat with a veil, being supported by the Silver Fox, sombrely dressed in a dark suit and tie, leaving the service, visibly distressed.

I carried that image round in my head for months, imagining her tears. What must she have thought? Would there forever be a gap in her life? She's still in her thirties, her whole life ahead of her, but can there ever be someone like me again?

Impossible. But it doesn't stop me scrutinising the gossip columns and the announcement pages of the British press from afar, torturing myself that she's decided to settle for second best and is about to announce her engagement to some unworthy, unrighteous moron who couldn't possibly deserve her.

Why do I miss her so much? Was it the sex? Well, that goes without saying. She was the only woman I ever met who knew without fail when to be a goddess – slow, languorous, divine in her sensuality – and when to be a porn star. She could do both, and did, but it wasn't just that. There was something more. Was she my soulmate? Of course not. I don't have a soul to mate with. But even so, it makes me think. She was the one woman who never bored me.

With others, it could take as little as a few hours, sometimes minutes, before I was mentally yawning and checking out, sometimes literally looking over their shoulder to try to spot someone – anyone – more interesting. They say we can always forgive those who bore us, but never those whom we bore. I don't know about that. If I was lucky it lasted weeks, even months, but that was rare. Even with my ex-wife. Especially with my ex-wife, which tells you just how ill-judged that relationship was. How many times was the sex just a form of displacement activity, a way of making time pass until I could do something more interesting, or at any rate lose myself someplace else, generally with chemical assistance? Probably most of the time. After the first thousand there's really little new that any woman has to offer you. I know. I'm shallow. Profoundly shallow. Shallow all the way through and then some. And no doubt psychologically and emotionally inadequate. I think you have to be to make it in investment banking. Maybe self-awareness at least makes me honest. That would put a positive spin on it. But with Two Livers it really was different. With her I was the one who had to do the running to keep up. She made me raise my game, made me think and, in the end, made me better. Or, less bad.

On reflection, being dead isn't much fun at all. Even dead rich doesn't help. This can't go on. In the long run we're all dust, so while we're here we need to do things. Real things. Eventually hedonism becomes boring. We need to be stretched and tested. At least I do. All my life I've struggled – well, relatively – and now I've got the pot of gold at the end of the rainbow, in fact a super-jumbo-sized one, I see just how worthless it is. Not that I'd ever give it back. But I want other things more now. Things I haven't got.

I need a nest. Banal as it sounds, I realise it's true. Or at least I think it is. Could I really settle down? Probably not for long. But with Two Livers there might be a chance.

A memory comes to mind. It was a Saturday afternoon, a couple of years ago now, and I was spending a lazy day at Two Livers' place in Mayfair. She had a giant-screen TV and I was flopped on a sofa watching a rugby international from Twickenham. England were kicking the arses of the Welsh. What happened next is as real today as it was when it happened, and I can still recall every detail.

Two Livers comes in, wearing a skimpy tennis outfit.

'How was your lesson?' I ask.

'Fab.' She leans forward and kisses me. 'I'm hot. I'm going to take a shower. Do you want a beer and a blow job first?'

'Sure. Why not?'

She disappears to the kitchen, where I hear the sound of a bottle top being removed, then comes back, hands me an ice-cold beer, kneels down, slips her top off and starts to unzip me.

'Oh, and after the match I want to run through my thoughts on the Asia-Pac conference.'

'The what . . . ?' I look at her, puzzled.

'The spring conference we're organising with business leaders from across the region. You're giving the keynote address. I've drafted your speech. You're going to say some radical things. They won't know what's hit them.'

'Radical? Oh . . . sure, great.'

Maybe a similar sort of thing was happening in millions of rugby-watching households up and down the country.

Then there was my birthday. I think it was the same year. We had dinner by ourselves at Restaurant Gordon Ramsay in Royal Hospital Road, Chelsea, still the best restaurant in London, and afterwards went to Mimi, off Berkeley Square, for a nightcap. Two Livers was wearing a vivid red 'look at me' cocktail dress by Zac Posen, with diamond cluster earrings by Graff, and predictably turned every head wherever we went. As did I, but only because they were all thinking, 'Who is that guy and how come he won the lottery?' That's where we 'bumped into' Anne-Marie Chantalle, the stunning nearest thing the French have to an equivalent of Two Livers, but brunette, with smaller breasts than Two Livers' perfect 34DDs and what the French call a 'gamine' air to her.

She was sitting alone at the bar drinking a champagne cocktail, wearing an Emilio Pucci peasant-style lace-up top that she'd left invitingly open at the front to show she was bra-less underneath, with tight knee-length leather boots and bare, tanned legs that were begging me to run my hand up them to discover whether she'd dispensed with underwear altogether for the evening. Anne-Marie runs a small investment banking boutique in Paris, and I'd wanted to hire her – and much more – for years.

There were squeals of 'surprise' from the two ladies, kisses on each cheek, more cocktails, then it was back to my apartment. I was in the kitchen opening another bottle – or was I scoring another sneaky line? – either way, when I came back into the living room the ladies were gone. I could hear them in the bedroom and quietly opened the door. They were naked, save for their jewellery – always a nice touch – and making out on my mega double bed. They looked up. Anne-Marie spoke first.

'The birthday boy. Come on, Dave. *Déshabille-toi.*'

What followed was one of the all-time great experiences of my life. So good, in fact, that I regretted the drink and the drugs, because I wanted to feel every second of it and imprint it on my memory forever. When they had finished with each other, they went to work on me. Together. But it was my birthday, and I suppose that Two Livers had simply organised the kind of treat that every girl does for her man on his birthday.

It was a memorable day. And if I have a chance of getting her back, it has to be worth a shot.

RETURNING FROM the dead is never straightforward.

I'm in, of all places, an opium den, when I realise how I'm going to do it. Or maybe it's because I'm there that I finally achieve clarity. Or something. Whatever it is, everything suddenly becomes clear.

I'm lying on a pile of silk cushions, smiling half-wittedly

at a beautiful Indonesian girl who is kneeling at my feet, her long hair tumbling down over her bare breasts, preparing me another pipe.

She has amazingly detailed, elaborate tattoos over most of her back and arms, and I find them utterly tantalising. I'm not normally an admirer of tattoos, especially on women. And I particularly despise the tasteless, vulgar slag tags and tramp stamps that British women go in for – some idiotic phrase in Sanskrit or ancient Greek, or some other language their under-educated brains wouldn't understand – located at the base of their back to remind you they're slappers when you're humping them from behind. Or worse still the twee 'discreet' little pictures that teenagers have somewhere on their bodies – flowers, dolphins or butterflies – normally hidden by clothing, so they can all show just how identically individual and daring and mysterious and sexy every single one of them is – in exactly the same way.

This is different. This really is extraordinary. One could spend days exploring her body. Her skin is a work of art, and I could lose myself in it.

I inhale deeply from the fresh pipe that she hands me. The feeling of relaxation is total. Nothing matters any more. It isn't that I've forgotten everything; on the contrary, I can see it all perfectly clearly and I realise that none of it matters. Except perhaps one thing. The one thing I never conquered. Everything else I had, generally more than once, both good and bad. And it was all irrelevant compared to the one thing I never achieved. Happiness in love.

Christ, this stuff is good. I had to try it because it was on my list and I'd never done it before. I've now tried it three times, and this is definitely the last, because it's so good I'd happily surrender to it. You really don't need to try this stuff. Trust me, I've done it for you.

The girl moves her hand to my crotch.

'Would you like me to make you comfortable?'

'No. But thank you. You're very kind.' I decline as politely as I can, and just in case she's offended, or might be missing out on a money-making opportunity, I reach into my pocket and pass her an enormous wad of notes.

I've been on a kind of circuit: an international pleasure circuit. My money is stashed in thirty or more banks around the world: small private banks in Russia and Central Asia; discreet wealth managers from Monaco to Macao; commercial banks in places most people have never heard of, like Nauru, that well-known global financial centre located on a tiny island in the Pacific, where even today few questions are asked if the numbers are large enough.

And I've been moving from place to place, sometimes in private jets, sometimes by luxury yacht, rarely coming into contact with the great unwashed whose money was needed to finance all this.

There are hundreds of people like me, doing the circuit. Occasionally we glimpse each other, arriving and leaving from private islands, boarding helicopters or landing from inflatables on remote coral atolls. A few I recognise, most I don't. Drug lords, Mafiosi, retired politicians and, of course, businessmen and 'failed' bankers. Even the occasional rock star whose albums I used to buy. People who made money that they would rather not see exposed to the police or the taxman, a whole class of super-rich 'disappeared' people, a number of them, like me, long since officially declared dead, but all of them using up time, wandering aimlessly and pleasurably, and waiting to die.

Well, not me. Not any more. The great thing about opium is the way it shifts the gears in your brain. Obstacles, baggage and general clutter disappear before its easily smoothing logic.

So now I know what I have to do.

BANG BANG Lee is surprised to get my call.

'Dave, is that you? No. Not Dave. You sounded like someone else. Let me think. Is it . . . ?'

He's forgotten. How could he? He's forgotten my chosen alias.

'It's Freddie, Bang Bang. Your old friend, Fred the Bed. Do you remember me?'

'Of course, Freddie. You just sounded like someone else. But I thought ...'

'You thought I'd decided to retire. Well, I had a change of heart. Now Freddie's going to retire instead. Permanently. And I heard that Dave's coming back. Think of him as the Comeback Kid. And he tells me he's going to need some help from you and Rom, and some of your friends.'

There's a long pause at the other end of the line. He owes me big time, and deep down he is a man of honour. At least a kind of honour. But our deal is over, finished, and he never expected to hear from me again. In fact that was my side of the bargain. I imagine the cogs in his head whirring. He's probably wondering whether it would be easier to make me disappear permanently, only to do it for real this time. On the other hand, the last time we worked together it was hardly boring. I need to dangle some bait.

'Bang Bang, we have unfinished business.'

'What do you mean?'

'I mean what we left on the table. We came away too soon. We never played the second-half.'

'The second-half?'

'Well . . . it's not exactly half. It's more than half.'

'Da— I mean Freddie – are you saying that we could have made more than we already did? That there's still more profit to take?'

'That's exactly what I'm saying. I've had time to reflect and it's all clear to me now. We were fools.' Fools who made billions. He's probably thinking that kind of foolishness is perfectly acceptable.

Silence. I wonder if we've been cut off. 'Bang Bang – are you there?'

'I'm here. When you see Dave, tell him he has my full attention.'

THE THING about people like Bang Bang and Rom is they can make things happen. Like the giant Russian Antonov aircraft that only just fits on the runway of the tiny Indonesian island where I've been put ashore.

Nothing this size has ever landed here before. It's a long-range cargo version, but its only cargo is an elaborate oversized caravan that's been driven into the hold of the aircraft, the sort movie stars live in on location, and which redefines luxury and excess, full of leather and fur and gilt and general vulgarity. It's for me and it's full of champagne, caviar and blondes. Well, and a few brunettes. And a couple of Asian girls – as if I haven't had enough – and a truly stunning black girl, who could be the first course of my in-flight entertainment. Even the president of the United States doesn't get this on Air Force One. As far as I know. I'm sure if he did, we'd have heard about it.

The only detail missing is Alessandro and the team from Duke's to pour the martinis. That would have been the perfect touch, with a bar set up in the hold of the aircraft. But I can't have everything – not yet. Anyway, it's going to fly me halfway round the world, and I climb aboard with a spring in my step. I'm coming home.

I THINK the girls must have been acting under instructions, because after a couple of hours I find myself yawning, glance suspiciously at the half-filled glass of champagne beside me, which doesn't taste quite right, and drift off to sleep. They don't wake me until we're about an hour out from our destination, a disused military airfield in Kazakhstan. I've got a very important meeting with my business partners, and then I'm going to have a video conference with the Silver Fox, though he doesn't know it yet.

For the size of aircraft, the landing is surprisingly smooth. Whoever the pilots are, they really know their stuff. We land and I say goodbye to the girls and walk down a huge ramp at the rear of the aircraft that opens to let in the scorching, dry heat of summer on the Kazakh steppe.

I'm wearing Bermuda shorts and a floral Hawaiian shirt that I picked up somewhere on my travels, and as I see the welcoming committee lined up before me, I suddenly feel underdressed.

On one side of the ramp, Bang Bang Lee is standing with a line of extras from *Kill Bill*, all in their identical dark Armani suits with black ties and Ray-Bans.

On the other side, Rom Romanov is visibly suffering in the heat, huge and impassive, his unnaturally dark hair looking even more slicked back than usual. He's wearing a crumpled sweat-stained grey suit whose tailor would no longer recognise it, his pale skin gleaming with a sheen of perspiration. Alongside him, his even huger bodyguards appear to be suffering more than their boss. I wonder if they were all flown out here in deep freeze units and have been awakened specially for me.

And then there are the others, the ones I never met first time round. There are South American types, Middle Easterners, Indians, more Chinese and, of course, Italians – easily the best dressed – plus a few I can't place. They look as if they really shouldn't all be together in one place and, if they are, then at least they shouldn't be seen out in the open. Somewhere up there a satellite is wondering what on earth is happening.

I count nine private jets – in my banking days we called them smokers – lined up along the tarmac. No one else is in sight. No airport workers, ground staff, flight crews, just a long empty runway, hangars and a control tower, and us. Exclusive? It's beyond platinum class.

Bang Bang steps forward, takes off his sunglasses and stretches his arms wide to embrace me.

'Dave. It's been a long time. But you're looking good. Very good. Being dead obviously suited you.'

I smile and squeeze him tightly. 'Me being alive is going to suit us all much better, believe me.'

INVESTMENT BANKERS are used to being persuasive. Being persuasive is actually our principal professional skill. Forget numbers. Juniors can do numbers, and juniors are a commodity that you can buy by the yard. Persuasiveness, on the other hand, generally has to be bespoke; you cannot commoditise it, and it requires wisdom, judgement and experience. Yeah, right. What I'm saying is that we're ace bullshitters. It's what we do.

So sitting at the head of a makeshift table in an aircraft hangar, staring at a bunch of sceptical faces owned by some of the world's most successful – and therefore ruthless – criminals, without even the benefit of some Powerpoint bullshit to hide behind, doesn't faze me at all. In fact, I love it so much I can feel something starting to run through my veins that hasn't been there for a while – something that doesn't come in tablet form, powder or a syringe.

'Gentlemen – we left the table too soon. We made out like bandits,' I glance quickly around the table, 'if you'll forgive the term, when markets fell and we were short. Governments reacted as we thought they would, panicking, unable to respond in Wall Street time rather than Whitehall time. Or, even worse, Brussels and Washington time. And what they did do was too late and only fed the beast they were trying to tame. We cleaned up. It was wonderful.'

At this point I'm touched when Rom starts clapping. It's a little slow, as if he only manages it with a huge effort, and for a moment I think he's taking the piss, but the others join in and clearly they are showing their appreciation.

'Thank you.' I nod gratefully. Always a good sign when your audience clap before the end. 'But we chose that moment to close our positions, taking our profits and walking away.'

'No one ever lost money taking a profit.'

It's Carlos, a Venezuelan who I think bankrolls terrorists. Or maybe he's the white slaver. Whatever. They were all introduced in one go and I've never been a great one for detail.

'Absolutely right.' I nod my strong agreement. 'But we should have played the bounce. Not just closed the short, but bought the market and watched it go up as it recovered.'

'But it didn't recover.' Carlos is clearly a market expert.

'Correct again. Because we didn't make it recover. It was ready. It was oversold. But everyone was sitting on their hands, scared shitless. We were the only ones in the know and we could have made the running. We could have called the market and made it happen. We could have been the market. If you have enough size on your side, weight of money alone will make you a winner. We had it and we could have used it, but we didn't. We banked our profits and thought we'd done well. A few tens of billions between us. It was probably the stupidest thing we ever did. Gentlemen, we could have had more . . . an awful lot more.'

They're looking thoughtful now. Amazing. These gangsters made vast fortunes but still it wasn't enough. Worse than bankers.

'And we still could. There's still an opportunity. Markets are volatile, fragile, out of control. Governments are almost all in deficit, but some of them are cutting spending and scaring everyone that they'll push the world into recession. While they're doing that, others are printing money and pumping it into the economy in an attempt to get things going again – but risking their currencies and running up debts their grandchildren will still be paying. And everyone hates the banks. Bastards. Just because we were greedy, overpaid parasites who were running out of control. We had the party, but everyone else had the hangover. And now the politicians all want to go banker-bashing and the regulators are licking their lips and planning how to carve up the banks. I never did like regulators – little mean guys with no charisma who never got paid properly.' I shrug and look helplessly at Carlos. 'It's a nightmare.'

'But where does our profit come from?'

'Oh, the profit? That's easy.' I scan the faces around the table. 'Isn't it obvious?'

None of them wants to speak. They may have some thoughts, but none of them wants to look stupid in front of the others.

'I go back. I return from the dead. I set up a fund to trade the markets again – a comeback fund, a salvation fund. Very high profile, because the best place to hide wrongdoing in the markets is in plain sight. And do it large. This will be a fund that backs the recovery, and more than that: creates the recovery. And when this fund puts on positions, guess what? A whole bunch of other guys place the same bets. Think weight of money. We'll be like a sumo wrestler playing with six-stone weaklings. Our bets will be so successful that, after a while, everyone will follow us. Just making a bet will mean it's a success as soon as people know about it. In the old days this was called market manipulation, but that was only if you got caught. And we won't get caught, because we'll have our own firm. We'll buy one. A small one, but very high calibre. And we'll only employ totally trustworthy people. Our own people. Everyone here can nominate someone. We won't need many because the settlement and back office side are automated; all we need is someone to take the decisions on the trades that we'll make, and that'll be me. Our target will be to double our money in six months. We'll start with, say, ten billion or so and take it from there. I suggest we stop when we hit fifty, but we can decide that later.'

I relax and sit down, a modest smile on my face. 'So . . . who wants to play?'

I do have a moment of nervousness as the silence stretches out for one, two, almost three seconds before the magic kicks in. First one, then another, then all of them start nodding. One or two are actually rubbing their chins, licking their lips, taking cautious sips of water from the glasses in front of them. I've got them. I love these moments. But there's one final detail – an important one if I'm ever to have a chance of winning Two Livers.

'One final point . . .' I begin.

'What's that?' It's Bang Bang, and he knows me well enough to see that a key moment is coming. 'Are you going to talk to us about the way the profit is split?'

Every eye is on me. They think I'm making a big play for more of the upside. They're wrong. It's worse than that.

'No. That stays the same.' They all relax, a few of them even smile. 'I want something much more important than that.'

'What's more important than money?' It's Carlos, unable to resist taking the floor again. Fucking tango dancer.

I look around the table, staring at each of them in turn. 'When this is over and we've all made billions more than we ever dreamt possible, you have to give me your word about one thing.'

You can hear the proverbial pin drop in the hangar.

'All of you – and your people, your organisations, your cartels, everyone you control . . .'

Now they're straining on my every word. The tension is killing them.

'All of you will promise never to do anything bad again. Ever.'

'WHAT?' It's Rom, but he could be speaking for all of them. 'Are you crazy? Are you joking?'

Carlos intervenes, half apologetic. 'Dave, we aren't going to stop doing . . . let's say, our *normal business*. It's what we do. It's how we put meat on the table.'

I stare at him evenly, trying not to be provocative, trying to hide whatever I might really think of him.

'Carlos, this is different. This time we're all going to make so much money that we'll actually stand to make more and do better and have more fun by going straight once it is over. Think billions, Carlos. Billions and billions. '

'But we're bad people. That's who we are. It's what we do. We're like bankers, only criminals. Look what you guys did. Far worse than us. No one ever asked you to stop being bankers. No prison. They even kept on paying you.'

I shrug sympathetically. 'I know. But bankers are different. And after this, everything will be transformed – for all of us. And I am serious. Is everyone on board?'

RUNNING A video conference from the middle of the Kazakh steppe requires some serious equipment. Luckily, that's exactly what we have. A team of technicians have set up something that looks like a TV studio in one of the hangars. I'm sitting at a desk, looking almost like a newsreader, waiting to be connected to the offices of Ball Taittinger in London. The Silver Fox thinks he's got a new business call with a client from the Far East. In a sense, he has.

When he comes into the room I've set the screen so that I can see what's happening at his end, but he can't yet see me. He looks remarkably unchanged, in a snappy Savile Row suit, pale pink Hermès tie and with his silver-grey hair swept back off his perma-tanned face. For a man in his sixties, he's handsome, dashing and sophisticated – the kind of operator you'd expect to run the best public relations firm in the business.

'You're looking good.'

He stares at the screen, gets only a screensaver rather than a face and looks to his left, presumably at the technician running the conference at his end.

'I'm sorry, who is this?'

I flick a switch and savour the impact. It takes a second, as he switches back to the screen, and then zooms in on my face.

'Is . . . this . . . a joke? Or a recording? What's going on?'

I chuckle in response to his remark and he almost leaps out of his chair. It's the first and only time I can ever recall him totally flummoxed. I have to put him out of his misery.

'Neither. It's me. I'm here. I'm alive and I'm well. And I'm coming back. To do that I'm going to need to hire a good PR firm. The best. I don't care what they charge me, but they have to be good. Because I'm coming back from the dead. Let's talk about your firm's credentials. How many people have you brought back from the dead?'

Even the smartest pro in the business takes a little while to get over that one. But to give him full credit, once he's heard my amazing story – the way I was fished out of the Thames by a passing barge, resuscitated, and then stayed on board, recovering, until they reached the Channel, where I transferred to a cargo ship and decided just to disappear – he rolls remarkably fast with the punches. In no time at all he's suggesting ways I can emphasise certain aspects of my 'time away', as he calls it, like the months I spent in a Tibetan monastery, meditating and reflecting on life's values, the charitable work I did in Chinese orphanages and, of course, the time devoted to prayer. Oh, and he also says how pleased he is to have me back. And you know what? I think he actually means it.

IT'S AMAZING how much you can get done, even from the Kazakh steppe, when you have unlimited money and some of the best people in the world working for you. I'm a fortnight into my stay here and already I have a credible alibi for where I've been and what happened after Blackfriars Bridge. Around the world more than fifty financial institutions have quietly started accumulating positions in companies that might turn out to have a more interesting future ahead of them than they realise right now. Because you never know what the future might hold.

In London, a hotshot investment banker called Laura MacKay is surrounded by an invisible aura. Invisible and protective. She's done fantastically well in the crisis, keeping Grossbank afloat, holding it together without selling out to either the British or German governments, but working the kind of hours that would kill a mere mortal and having very little time to play. As her reward, they've made her chairman. My old job. It couldn't be in better hands, though I guess it's been a killer.

Which is not to say she's been totally idle. At one time she was dating a well-known Indian millionaire playboy, but just in the last couple of days his family have called him home to Mumbai to marry the daughter of another wealthy Indian dynasty. Apparently, they've signed a mega deal with a brand-new but very influential Asian industrial conglomerate that came out of nowhere, and the other

30

side specified that he had to come home, settle down and take the reins.

Miss MacKay was also seen out a couple of times with a Chelsea footballer, but just in the last week he's been sold for a record price to a team in Tajikistan that no one's ever heard of, but which a local oligarch has apparently decided to turn into a Champions' League side.

And she was photographed in a celebrity magazine with an up-and-coming actor, a good-looking guy with pecs and shoulders and a hero's jaw. But he's just landed a breakthrough role in a major feature film that had a financing package come through unexpectedly from some Latin American business tycoon. He starts shooting next week in Patagonia – for six months.

So she's all alone, but around her wheels are in motion, and although she doesn't know it, she's never really alone. An invisible cordon surrounds her, electronically, digitally and, at a discreet distance, physically, all of the time. No one can mug her, no one can molest her, no burglar will get near her home. Even the secret service couldn't provide better protection. All they can do is arrest the bad guys. The people watching Two Livers *are* the bad guys. Fuck with them and they'll put two bullets in the back of your head – and they don't need to trouble anyone with questions. She's safe, looked after on my behalf until I return home, and I need to get cracking.

Before the world can know I'm still around, she has to. I don't want to speak to her on the telephone – I need to see her face. I don't want to con her into a video conference. However good the technology, I need to feel her reaction, sense it, live it, in a way that only works if you are physically there alongside her. Sneaking into the country is a high-risk move, but luckily I have powerful friends in low places.

So on a dull, overcast Saturday morning I find myself standing outside a coffee shop on Oxford Street, furtively looking at a reflection in the window from the other side of the road. It's her. She's wearing a Vivienne Westwood blazer and, what I guess, are J Brand jeans. She has a Tod's handbag casually slung over her shoulder and large sunglasses that I like but can't place. She's walking fast, her pace confident, and has a 'don't fuck with me' look on her face that discourages admiring glances from the men she passes in the street.

I've been following her for nearly twenty minutes, having picked her up outside her home, a large Mayfair townhouse that she must have bought since getting the top job at Grossbank. I'm wearing a donkey jacket and jeans, dark glasses, a blue baseball cap with its peak pulled down at the front, and I haven't shaved for a week. It's my idea of a disguise, but it seemed better as an idea than it looks in practice. In the movies the guys on the surveillance team never stand out, even when they lurk in doorways or hang around on street corners. In real life I feel like I've got a flashing light on my head and a klaxon going off just in case she doesn't notice me.

She turns off Oxford Street, crosses Wigmore Street and heads up Harley Street. It's long and open, largely residential or offices, mostly occupied by expensive medical practices. I cross to the other side of the road and observe her as we walk almost the full length of the street, until she stops and pauses at a large front door, goes up the steps and rings the bell. After a moment the door opens and she goes inside. Then I realise where she is. It's the Foetal Medicine Centre. I came here with Wendy when she was expecting Samantha. And on another occasion early on in my marriage, much more discreetly, with someone else. That didn't have a happy ending.

Two Livers must be pregnant. How did it happen? Well, I can guess *how* it happened. But when? And with whom? She was supposed to be under proper surveillance. Does this mean she's in love? She'd never be pregnant by accident. I have a sick feeling in my stomach and suddenly start questioning everything. There must be someone else. Someone I don't know about.

Which is when she suddenly reappears and heads across the street directly towards me. I pretend to look at my watch, turn round to glance at a street sign, then catch my breath as I hear her footsteps behind me.

'I thought you were supposed to be dead?'

That voice. Deep, husky, unhurried. One of the sexiest voices I can recall. I turn to face her, feeling like a schoolboy caught with his fingers in the biscuit tin. Before I can reply, she continues.

'I never believed it. There were moments, like the memorial service, when I missed you more than you can ever believe. But I always knew you were too selfish to kill yourself. There had to be a plan. It had to be another of your schemes.' She's shaking her head, looking down at the pavement, sad and for a moment, lost. 'You're too arrogant to believe the world could ever do without you.'

I take my sunglasses off and stare at her, willing her to do the same so that our eyes can meet. Windows on the soul. I need to see what she's truly feeling.

'When did you spot me?'

She shakes her head again, despairing. 'Don't apply for MI6.'

'Was I that bad?'

'Worse.' For a moment I think she's going to laugh, her deep, throaty, loving-life, 'come to bed' laugh that I've ached to hear. But she doesn't. And the sunglasses stay on.

'I came back . . . for you. I missed you too much. It was all so empty without you.'

'Sure you did, Dave. If you missed me at all, it was because you didn't have me anymore. If you'd really cared, I'd have been part of the plan and gone with you. I would have, you know.'

My gut is twisting with guilt, anguish, desperate frustration and a dozen other feelings that make me feel as if I'm going to explode.

'Is there . . . a chance?'

'I don't know.'

I step forward, wanting to embrace her, but she raises a hand to keep me away.

'First you have to come back from the dead. How are you going to do that?'

'I've got a plan.'

Now she does laugh, but it's a short, dismissive, angry laugh. 'I bet you have. You always have a plan. You'll find some changes.'

'What sort of changes?'

'The City is different. The little people are in charge now – the regulators, the risk managers, the bean counters. They're having their moment in the sun.'

'And Grossbank?'

'I run the bank now.'

That much I knew.

She sighs. 'And it's bigger.'

It is. She's acquired some of the bank's smaller competitors in Germany and elsewhere, using Grossbank's muscle to take advantage of hard times for the small fry.

'You've done a great job hoovering up the little guys, growing the firm. Everything I hear is good.'

'The little guys were like a bunch of drunks propping each other up in a bar. It was easy. And besides, I had a good teacher.'

'If you mean me, I love to be praised, but I think you did the teaching – to me. You and Paul.'

'Who?'

'You know who. Paul Ryan – what happened to him?' Paul would have expected to become co-head alongside her. He was head of Markets whereas she ran Corporates – together the two most powerful people in the firm after me. Paul turned on me at the end, smelling the chance to grab the reins for himself.

'Dead.'

'Dead?'

'Not literally. I fired him. You can't have more than one queen bee in a hive. That much I did learn from you.'

'How did you fire him? He must have put up a fight.'

She nods. 'Took me almost a week.'

'Good. Serves him right. Wanker.'

Two Livers offers no further comment. Enough said. This woman is impressive. Chairman and saviour of one of the biggest banks in the world and not yet forty, a rock star performance that dwarfs anything I ever did.

I nod towards the doorway across the street. 'Just now . . . were you . . . ?'

Finally, she throws her head back and gives a rich and

throaty laugh. I want to hug her, but I hold back.

'I thought that would scare the shit out of you,' she says.

'So, you're not . . .' I gesture towards her stomach.

'Not as far as I know. And I think I would know.'

Phew. I hope I don't show it, but the relief is overwhelming. She laughs again, tossing her head back with a characteristic gesture that I've dreamt about for months. She can read me like a book.

'Can I see you again?'

'Sure. I'm on CNBC and Bloomberg TV most weeks.'

'I mean . . . *see* you.'

There's a moment of sickening silence. Women never forgive. I left her. There's no escaping the fact. The tension hangs in the air as she removes her sunglasses, and I'm hugely, massively, overwhelmingly relieved to see tears in her eyes. Tears of happiness, or just tears?

'Maybe. I'll think about it. Come back from the dead first.'

I'VE MADE some grand entrances before, but there's something about dead people showing up that grabs the attention of the media in a particularly intense way. The first reporters are actually on the Air Astana flight from Almaty, having been prepped by the Silver Fox, and I give them 'exclusives' on the basis that they've already had a lot of advance briefing in London and are going to be friendly. Heathrow, by contrast, is a media scrum, with hundreds of photographers, cameramen and reporters shouting questions at me while I smile and give a friendly wave on my way to the press conference.

When we get to the actual briefing room, a huge, characterless auditorium filled with rows of cheap plastic chairs, it is packed, standing room only. The Silver Fox has dispensed with the usual desk covered with microphones, to hide behind, and opted instead for a simple canvas director's chair, where I sit alone and face the world. There are no Powerpoints on the wall behind me, no slides or photographs, nothing that smacks of preparation or slick presentation. I'm dressed in a neutral pale grey suit from a tailor in Almaty, neither sharp nor conservative, a collarless white cotton shirt unbuttoned at the top and grey canvas slip-on shoes with no socks. My hair is cut short. Nothing pretentious, nothing investment-banker-like, just simplicity, modesty – the kind of authenticity that comes from discovering who you are and being in touch with yourself and your inner values. And having a good PR adviser.

The Silver Fox stands at the front with a hand-held mic and addresses the crowd, some two hundred strong.

'Ladies and gentlemen, Mr Hart has just got off a long flight from Kazakhstan, and so this press conference will be kept short. You all have the press release and the detailed background notes, embargoed until the end of today's session. Mr Hart will be available over the coming days to speak to many of you individually, but for today he is simply going to make a short statement about his plans for the future.'

This is smart. The tedious stuff about the Tibetan monastery and the Chinese orphanage, where I might have been tripped up on the detail, are dealt with in the handouts. In real life, Bang Bang has made some real monks and a real orphanage extremely happy – and extremely well briefed – in case some enterprising reporters go there to get the inside story.

There's a predictable hubbub, but he calms them down and passes the mic to me.

'Thank you. A lot of us wonder what will be said about us after our deaths. Only a few of us get to find out.' That gets a laugh. 'I know many of you will be wondering what happened to me these past months, where I've been and how is it that I suddenly appeared after so long, when many people thought I was dead. In fact, when everyone thought I was dead. At times even I thought I was dead.' Another laugh. A self-deprecating smile in response. 'I'll tell the full story in due course. What I want to focus on is not what happened to me. That's personal and, in the long run, irrelevant. I want to look at the big picture, at what happened to all of us.'

Like all investment bankers I'm much happier dealing with the big picture. Detail is dangerous. Detail trips you up. Detail is a four-letter word.

'I also want to talk about responsibility. When I jumped off Blackfriars Bridge I wanted to take responsibility – and face the consequences – for failure. I had failed. We all had failed in the financial community. I felt it was right that I should pay the price for what had happened, at least in so far as it affected my firm and the people, the livelihoods, that depended on me. I had done my best in impossible and unprecedented circumstances, and it wasn't enough. So I decided to take my own life. And I fully intended to do so. But fate intervened.'

'Many of you have heard already about the extraordinary circumstances that occurred on the night I jumped from the bridge. I was rescued from the water that I thought would be my last resting place. I believed it was game over. Instead, I was taken on a journey that would change my life. A journey that has taken me across the world and from which I have returned a changed man. A man who no longer thinks of himself, who has learnt values of a different kind from the ones he used to live by. And a man with the courage to return and attempt to rebuild, to repair the damage done by the old ways, to make good the harm he and others like him have caused.'

They are scribbling away, but still someone shouts out from the crowd, apparently breaking the convention of first identifying themselves. 'What does that mean, Mr Hart? What are you actually going to do?'

The guy's a plant, organised by the Silver Fox, because I don't have time to waste on drivel about my 'journey' and finding my inner self. I want tomorrow's story to be the super fund that's going to turn the world economy around.

'What am I going to do? I'm going to raise a fund – I call it the Salvation Fund – that will mobilise capital on a scale never previously attempted, and invest to undo the damage caused by the crash. It will be huge and, if I succeed as I intend, it will have a profound impact on all of our lives.' Most especially mine. Oh, and along the way I'll become a saint and get the girl, but we needn't go into that now.

A forest of hands go up and I look to see who the Silver Fox is looking at.

'Yes?' I meet the glance of a grey-haired reporter in the front row, a face I think I remember from television.

'Mark Foster, BBC *Financial Insight* – Mr Hart, what kind of fund do you have in mind? How big will it be? And what will it do?'

I pause, as if I have to reflect on my answer, giving due weight and gravitas to his question.

'I'm going to do something that I don't think has

ever been done before. I'm going to raise a private fund that will invest specifically in order to support global economic growth and prosperity. In the past, investing institutions didn't care where their money went, just as long as the returns were good. The hedge fund community was particularly notorious. They could sell a company's shares and bring it to its knees, or they could boost its stock price and send it through the roof – they didn't care. All they wanted was returns. I'm going to be different. I'm going to produce returns, of course – but I'll be doing it in a way that helps to turn the global economy around, taking risks to support the businesses that will help us grow our way out of trouble. And without being immodest, I don't think anyone understands the financial markets the way I do.'

I check with the Silver Fox and nod to a woman in the second row.

'Melanie Crowther, *Evening Post*. Mr Hart, how do you know you'll be able to raise a fund like this? These are hard times and money is in short supply. And you've just come back after, let's just say, a period of absence. What if you can't find people to back you?'

'Melanie, one thing I've come to believe is that if you do the right thing, you'll get the backing you need. I'm confident I can present a proposition for investors so compelling that they'll be queuing out the door. I anticipate raising ten billion dollars – minimum. For the first closing. Probably more later.'

More laughter, and a few shaking heads. The more financially astute think I've lost it. Too much time in the sun or doing yoga with monks. They wouldn't doubt me if they knew who was really waiting in the wings.

'One more question?'

They all go mad. They want to ask about my personal journey rather than the stuff that might make the finance pages. I follow the Silver Fox's eye and nod to a young woman reporter standing at the back.

'Jill Fairfax, *Finance Magazine*. Mr Hart, how will you judge whether your fund is successful?'

Another respectful pause. 'I'll double it. In a year, maybe less. Maybe six months. And I'll do it by backing winners, not by preying on the weak and the suffering. I'll do it by investing for good.'

The Silver Fox is on his feet, thanking them, pointing them towards more piles of handouts and ushering me out of the room. Tomorrow's headlines should start the ball rolling. Tomorrow is Day One. That gives me a hundred and eighty more, give or take, to make a fortune and save the world.

I HEAD towards the Ritz, where I've taken a suite on a long-term arrangement. The Ritz is classic, rather than trendy – it still has an irritating dress code – and it certainly isn't cheap, which helps to keep out the riff-raff. On the other hand, they really understand service, which is important for me because I don't want to do anything even vaguely domestic – ever. Plus they're conveniently located on Piccadilly in the heart of hedge fund world, and just around the corner from Duke's. When I get there they already know who I am, greet me by name and make me feel like I'm a long-lost member of the family who's just come home – the prodigal Mr Hart.

My possessions were all packed up and placed in storage while my ex-wife disputed the terms of my will. The Silver

Fox asks if I want him to arrange to get them out of storage. But why would I? In order to have belongings you need to belong. I don't belong anywhere.

More alarmingly, he's also dealing with the police. It seems they want to interview me, and not just because they're star-fuckers. He threatens them with a thousand kinds of hellfire and they back off, at least for now. As if I didn't have the right to try to take my own life. It's their fault if they wasted time investigating it. The good thing about having the Silver Fox speaking on your behalf is that he's the man who advised the commissioner of the Metropolitan Police on that little personal matter that none of us needs to know about.

Britain has changed since I went away. There's a coalition government. Whoever would have thought it? Liberal Democrats used to be able to indulge in free-thinking about impossible policies the proper parties wouldn't go near. Now they have responsibility, accountability, the pressures of office. Worse still, they're in power as the junior partners of a bunch of young, desperately inexperienced Old Etonian Conservatives, who believe in nothing except being very tough about whatever it is they don't believe in.

So the country has been plunged into a regime of austerity, cuts, general discomfort and, of course, banker bashing – we caused it all, after all, with our unbridled greed. Unbridled? Naturally – anyone who had a chance of making what we could as quickly as we could would have been daft not to go for it. Fucking hypocrites. It had nothing to do with the regulators, who were asleep at the wheel and saw nothing, knew nothing, and even if they had wouldn't have had a clue what to do about it. And it certainly wasn't the politicians' fault. They really were ignorant. Still are, in fact, except for a few new sound bites in the briefing pack from Central Office. Ignorance didn't stop them cosying up to the City when they thought that was where the money was, holding their hands out for contributions to the party and dangling knighthoods and ermine in front of the people who controlled the purse strings. And nor will it stop them in the future. Memories are short and it won't take long to get back to normal.

The challenge for me will be to distinguish myself from the rest of the City. Although, that shouldn't be too difficult. I've spent most of my career doing it, after all.

TO DO what I plan to do, I need to hire a law firm. Not just any law firm. The sheer scale of the undertaking, simultaneously in markets across the globe, is going to stretch the resources of any firm. So I'm not only hiring the best, I'm hiring the biggest.

DLR Strummer is the biggest law firm in the world. They're so big you could fill a small stadium with their lawyers. They're the legal equivalent of *Star Trek*'s Borg: relentless, virtually indestructible, and they're almost everywhere on the planet. It may be that they haven't yet opened in Antarctica, but as soon as they sniff a deal or spot a likely client, they'll be there. And, just like the Borg, when they come up against a competitor, they either destroy them or absorb them. Anyone who's any good ends up being part of DLR Strummer – individuals, teams, entire firms. Eventually, they could be the only law firm in the world.

As I contemplate what's going to happen next, I'm certain of one thing – size matters. If you're going to war, you want a Panzer Division on your side, not a troop of Boy Scouts.

When I speak to their managing partner about what I'm planning, he asks what I'll need from them.

'Here in London I want your biggest lawyers. Bring them in from wherever you have to. Cost is irrelevant. I want impact.'

'Our biggest? You mean our most senior, high-profile people – the "names" in the legal world? Or the ones who've worked on the very largest transactions?'

'Neither. I want physically large lawyers. Huge ones. I'll pay double the rate your partners charge for all the lawyers you've got who are over six foot three, regardless of seniority. Men or women. And I'll want them to wear Ray-Bans. Even indoors. In every meeting with our target companies. It's a personal quirk of mine. When I enter a meeting room I want people to think the Godfather's arrived. I want them to look at my legal team and think that if they don't sign, these guys could throw them out the window.'

I NEED an office and a trading platform, ideally a hedge fund type of operation trading all kinds of securities round the clock in markets across the world, staffed by some pretty high-calibre people who don't need me backseat driving all the time.

Mike Fisher runs Caveman Associates, a London-based hedge fund with about three billion dollars of assets investing in what they describe as a global macro strategy, spotting big trends and following them. Why did they call it Caveman? Because they could. They left larger, more conservative firms to set up on their own, and in these politically correct times the name made a statement. I've met Fisher socially a few times but can't call him a friend. Can I actually call anyone a friend? Good question.

I go to see him at his offices in Curzon Street, Mayfair, in a smart, high-tech building. Why do so many hedge funds base themselves around here? I have no idea, but simply observe that it's very handy for whatever pleasures Shepherd Market allegedly has to offer.

Fisher sits at a huge glass desk, surrounded by screens, in a large glass-walled corner office that looks out into his trading room, where a dozen traders are speaking into cordless earpieces and staring at even more screens. On one side of the trading room is a coffee 'pod', where the troops can help themselves to soft drinks and sandwiches, and next to it a pool table and a table tennis table. It's all a terrible cliché, but I love it.

Right now, two of DLR Strummer's finest are standing next to the coffee pod, dwarfing one of the traders who's gone for a refill, silently intimidating in their suits and ties and dark glasses. Reservoir Dogs meets the hedge fund industry.

Mike Fisher is mid-thirties, average height, balding and slightly stooped – too much time in front of computer screens. He learnt his trade on the proprietary trading desk at Hardman Stoney and left with three buddies to start their own firm five years ago. They haven't looked back. We sit down in his office and wait while an eye-candy babe pours coffee.

'So, Mr Hart – you've made quite a comeback.'

He points to the newspapers and magazines strewn across his desk. The headlines read, 'Back From The Dead' and 'Hart Returns to Save Markets'. I made a gratifying number of front pages.

'Call me Dave. I've come to buy your firm.'

To his credit, he doesn't blink. 'It's not for sale.'

I reach into my jacket pocket. Given my history, he does briefly look nervous about what I might have in there. Instead of whatever it was he was fearing, I take out a cheque and slide it across the table. His eyebrows go up.

'You really want to buy my firm.'

I glance out at my legal team standing by the coffee machine. 'And you really want to sell it.'

He follows my eyes and nods. 'I do? Oh, I see. Maybe I do. This is an impressive number. Very impressive. Very fair.'

Very fair is investment banking speak for too much. It is too much. But I don't have time to waste.

I nod. 'And you can always start again. You're young and you have time. I, on the other hand, am in a hurry. I have no time. You see, I have to get a haircut.' I look at my watch. 'I have an appointment at Trumpers down the road in five minutes. I'll come back and sign when I'm done. My legal team will handle the paperwork.'

He looks at the guys by the coffee machine. 'You mean they're *really* lawyers?'

'DLR Strummer. They're also lawyers.'

ONCE A man has his base, his office and, in my case, his trading platform from which to sally forth into the world markets, he then requires something – or someone, rather – without whom he is incomplete: someone who understands his needs, supports him through the sweetness of success and the bitterness of failure, standing by him unquestioningly and tirelessly. No, not his wife – his secretary. I'm thinking of Maria, my half-German, half-English personal assistant at Grossbank, a middle-aged Grossbank lifer who supported me through thick – and at times I was really thick – and thin. And there were certainly thin times. In fact, my legacy to the firm she devoted her life to was the thinnest of all times. As Grossbank's answer to Brunhilde, she weathered every storm and rolled with every punch. And now I want her back, to work for me in my new venture. I call the switchboard and ask for Maria.

'Miss MacKay's office.'

Damn. That's the first I knew about who she was working for. Inevitable, I suppose. The new chairman would want to have the old chairman's PA on side. She knows where the bodies are buried.

'Maria?'

A pause. 'Mr Hart?'

'Yes, Maria, it's me. How are you? It's been quite a while.'

'Mr Hart, we thought you were dead.'

'Well, technically I was. But I'm back now. Maria, there's something I wanted to ask you. Something personal. Are you OK to talk?'

Cautiously now. 'Yes . . .'

'Maria, you can guess what I'm going to ask you. I want you to come and join me in my new venture. It's a fund. The Salvation Fund. You may have read about it in the press. We're going to run, oh, ten billion or so to start with. A lot more later. Haven't raised it yet, but we will. And I want the old team to be back together again.'

'Mr Hart, you are very flattering. But I have been at the bank a long time. I've never worked anywhere else.'

'Maria, how does a million pounds sound to you?'

Surprisingly, a million pounds sounds like a lot to a secretary. Even to the chairman's personal assistant. Of course she accepts. Who wouldn't? But I'm prepared to be even more generous.

'Maria, alternatively, if you prefer, I'll give you one per cent of everything we make. I'll be running the fund personally. People will be backing me and my judgement. It won't be one of those vanity comeback funds that ex-bankers try. I'll put everything into this one, Maria – my heart, my soul, my total commitment – and it'll be big and hugely successful. What do you think?'

A pause. 'One million pounds is a wonderful offer, Mr Hart. Thank you so much.'

Now there's a vote of confidence.

But at least I have her. My comfort blanket is almost complete, bar one key component. Tom, my driver, sharper than any London taxi driver, quick witted, resourceful, smart and physically tall and imposing – the perfect chauffeur for someone who needs to move fast and has a habit of pissing people off.

So my next call is to the driver's pool at Grossbank. Can you believe it? After I left, they tossed Tom into the pool. Bastards. As a pool driver, he could be told to drive any jumped-up teenage managing director who doesn't even have hairs on his chest. How could they?

When someone answers the phone, I just say it's 'a friend'. But when he picks up, he knows.

'Mr Hart, sir. How are you?'

'How did you know it was me, Tom?'

'I read the papers, saw you on the news. You've lost a bit of weight. Suits you. So when do I start?'

'Right now?'

There's a pause and I hear him shouting to someone across the room. 'Tell him to drive himself to the airport. I just quit. Better offer.'

MARKETS HAVE rallied on news of my return. Well, they've rallied. Whether it's coincidence I'm not sure. Anyway, positive news is a good thing if you're fundraising, which I am.

Fundraising for a new investment fund is never straightforward but post credit crunch it's for heroes and naive romantics only, especially a so-called 'first-time' fund. Investors don't like parting with their money at the best of times, but after some spectacular crashes and insolvencies in the hedge fund industry, and with so many of yesterday's finance rock stars washed-up, it's easier to be 'prudent' and do nothing than stick one's head above the parapet. So the custodians of the wealth of some of the world's richest people – the private bankers and wealth managers – tend to give people like me the brush-off. OK, so there's no one quite like me. But you get the picture.

Today I'm seeing a lady called Jackie Scott. She's mid-forties, serious, conservative, and she most definitely doesn't gamble with her clients' money. As a man, I admire women with good posture. No stooping. Walk tall and look the world in the eye. Jackie walks so tall and straight you'd think she had a broom handle up her arse. The firm she works for is Banque Arabe et Genevoise, a Middle-Eastern-backed joint venture with a large Swiss private bank. Conservatism is second nature to them, though in the last few years a lot of Arab and other new money piled into their coffers. In the finest Swiss tradition, they asked the minimum number of questions about where it came from – which is why she's shortly going to get a surprise.

I'm sitting in the kind of oak-panelled meeting room with thick carpets and fake Impressionist pictures that private bankers think inspire confidence in their clients. Because I'm meeting a woman, and because I want to unsettle her, I've brought two female members of my legal team from DLR Strummer, a pair of Amazons in their late twenties who look like they've walked straight off the set of the latest *X-Men* movie.

Once the coffee and the introductions are over – 'Really? Your legal team?' was probably the high point – we get down to business. I slide the inevitable Powerpoint presentation across the table but then ignore it and talk passionately about the need to turn the global economy around, the importance of profiting by taking risks to back winners rather than shorting and tearing value apart and, of course, about my own motivation in wanting to make amends for my past failings.

All of this is the last thing she wants to hear. I sense my legal team shifting uncomfortably in their seats and can almost read the thought bubbles over their heads that say, 'He's blowing it – cut the emotion and stick to the numbers. Be rational, compose yourself, take a deep breath and start again.' If I were rational I wouldn't be where I am today. For that matter, none of us would.

So Jackie listens uncomfortably, and when my passion and excitement get too much for her she flicks through the presentation, reading ahead to the end before I get there, which just encourages me to go off piste even more and prolong the whole session until eventually we overrun and her secretary comes to remind her she has another engagement.

'Thank you, Mr Hart – fascinating. I've got your card – Caveman Hart Associates . . .'

She laughs uncomfortably and looks at the Amazons to see if they'll join in – but they stay poker-faced, and even if they didn't have their shades on they'd give nothing away. She coughs nervously to hide her embarrassment.

'Mr Hart, we'll come back to you.' She shakes her head, half disbelieving. 'A number of our clients have already expressed interest in understanding what you're planning to do next, just from what they've read about you in the press.'

'A little publicity never hurt.'

I smile, we shake hands and she shows us out, clearly never expecting me to darken her doors again.

I COULDN'T put her off forever. It was inevitable. Wendy. Wendy the ex, once known as Attila the Ex, until she was neutered with a deal whereby she thought she was fleecing me and took a pay-off just before I started making real money. Some you lose, some you lose. Bad luck, Wendy. She wants to see me to 'talk about Samantha'. Yeah right. Samantha means money. Samantha is Wendy's route to my wallet. Whatever it is Samantha needs, it's likely to mean Wendy will end up with a bigger house/car/holiday allowance/ski chalet, etc., etc. Wendy's the kind of ex-wife who gives ex-wives a bad name. On the other hand, maybe I'm the kind of ex-husband . . . Anyway, let's not go there.

Maria shows her in, pursing her lips and looking at the ceiling as if she has a bad smell under her nose. Maria never did like Wendy.

Wendy's made a real effort. She's wearing a pale blue matching skirt and jacket by Armani that shows off what

I'm guessing is a fake tan, with diamond and pearl white-gold earrings by Tiffany and a matching brooch. She has a white Gucci handbag and shoes by Jimmy Choo. It looks like she's had her hair done specially, the way she does most days of the week with a 'y' in them – and no doubt a mani/pedi, and probably a massage as well, though not that sort.

These middle-aged Chelsea women are amazing. They don't age. Maybe there's something in the air in SW3. Or maybe it's the water. No wrinkles, no crow's feet, no laughter lines, no furrowed brows worn with age and care. These women are truly ageless, neat, trim, nipped and tucked and shaped and sculpted and worked out to produce the best looks money can buy. My money can clearly stretch quite far.

So as soon as I see her I get up, concerned, and pull out a chair for her.

'Wendy – hey, come here and sit down. Are you OK?'

'Dave – of course. I'm fine. What's –'

'Are you sure? You look . . . well . . . Are you sure you're OK?'

'Yes, I'm OK. I'd know if I wasn't OK.'

'All right, I'm sorry. I guess I haven't seen you in a while. How are you?'

'I'm fine. Worried, about you and about all these things I read in the papers. And exhausted, having to explain to Samantha everything that's happened. She thought you were dead. We both did. You never even let us know. How could you?'

Easy. I'm a bastard. Utterly self-centred. I shake my head.

'I know.' Deep breath. 'It's been tough. Tougher than you can possibly imagine.'

There's a 'yeah right' thought bubble over her head. She

thinks she has me on the back foot and decides to press her advantage.

'When do you want to see her, by the way? She's your daughter, Dave, and she hardly knows you.'

'I'll get in touch as soon as my feet hit the ground. I'd love to see her, but right now I'm snowed under.' I point at the piles of papers on the desk, none of which I have any intention of reading. 'You can see how busy I am.'

'Of course, but don't you have people . . . ?'

'It's not the same. I'm starting out afresh. I have to get this right. It's not the bank anymore. This is me.' I look at her face as if I've spotted something. She follows my eyes and puts her hand to her forehead. 'Wendy, are you sure you're all right? You look . . . older?'

Her voice is icy now. 'We're all older, Dave. It's what happens.'

I hold up a hand apologetically, defensively. 'I know. I'm sorry. I guess it's just unfair how it works, you know ... with men and women.'

'What do you mean?'

'Oh, nothing. I was just thinking about that stupid cliché about men growing more distinguished as they get older and women just growing . . . Well, anyway, let's change the subject.'

The temperature in the room drops about ten degrees. Who needs air-con when you have an ex-wife? I like it this way.

'Let's. And by the way, you might be interested to hear I do have a new man in my life. I thought you should know, just in case it comes up when you see Samantha.'

Touché. As if I care.

'Wendy, that's fantastic. Maria! Maria – do we have a

bottle of champagne in the fridge? Wendy has some great news.'

Now she's blushing. At least I think it's a blush beneath the fake tan.

'It's not . . . It's not serious.' Couldn't be, otherwise he'd be the one writing the cheque for whatever it is she's come to see me about today.

'Maria – hold the champagne.' I turn back to Wendy. 'White wine instead? Or coffee? Water?'

'You know you have some grey hairs?' Meow.

'Dye.'

'What?'

I think she thinks I said, 'Die.'

'I dye it. Makes me look more distinguished. Gives me gravitas. Very important in some parts of the world – Asia, Middle East, Africa.'

From then on it's all downhill. She doesn't want to hear about my amazing adventures, 'finding myself' in the Himalayas, being adopted by a Tibetan guru, working with Chinese orphans, or whatever. Anyone would think she assumed I spent my time away shagging and doing drugs.

She wants more money for Samantha to have a bigger place in the country to go to at weekends, where her friends can come to stay and they can all ride ponies. She wants another new car – a two seater, because it's not practical to go everywhere in the S Class Merc I bought her last year to take Samantha on the school run, and there's a new Maserati that would make a perfect lady's car. And then she wants me to pay the bill for her probate lawyers. She had to contest my will for Samantha's sake, and now that I'm alive – for which we're all supremely grateful – they're expecting her to settle her account.

I'd like to say I showed her the door. I really should have. But because I'm a man, and therefore weak and gullible and prone to feelings of guilt as well as metaphysical anguish, I wrote her a large cheque. I'm not going to say how much. Large.

I GET a phone call from Jackie Scott at Banque Arabe et Genevoise. She doesn't quite know how to say this, but, well, they'd actually like to invest in the new fund. In size. She reported back to her clients who had specifically said to her they were interested in what I was up to, and the result was, well, unprecedented. Seven billion. From clients all over the world. And word spread and they even had some new clients – people they'd never dealt with before – who were investing with them for the first time precisely in order to have access to the Salvation Fund. It is the most she has ever seen invested in a single fund by the bank's clients, let alone a first-time fund with no specific track record.

She can only think that it is me people are backing. Clearly my name counts for a lot. My name and what I've been through. And, of course, she had personally been very impressed indeed and had passed that on to the bank's clients. It's not often a prospective fund manager speaks with such passion. Normally these presentations are such dry affairs, numbers driven and rather dull. So she likes to think she's contributed in some small way to my success, and can I remind her again what I'd said about rebating fees to introducers of investment funds? It's very rare for a private banker not to pay full attention to anything that relates to how they get paid, so she clearly hadn't rated my chances at all.

Over the next few days I get similar equally surprised calls from a dozen other banks and private wealth managers, all of them equally baffled. The total for the first closing of the Salvation Fund comes to eighteen billion dollars. Where was all this money coming from? How had I generated such interest?

Clearly it's my charisma. That and the fact that the world's largest organised crime organisations are collectively raiding their piggy banks on a scale they've never done before.

I HAVE a date. Well, not exactly a date. I'm meeting Two Livers for drinks. This is potentially dangerous because I still don't know what's going on in her head. Besides, she can famously drink for England, whereas I can't – I might manage Wales – and I've convinced myself that for the first time in my life I'm in love. I've also stolen her secretary.

I've decided that up to now I've been a user of women in the same way that I'm a user of Class A drugs – though arguably women do you more harm. Moments of ecstasy followed by huge downers, emotional and physical exhaustion, and a profound sense of emptiness. How many times have I asked myself: is that it? Is that what it's all about? And then there's that dangerous precipice, where you find yourself wondering if it could get any better – if you just went that little bit further, were a little more daring, greedier, more hedonistic – and of course you step forward and find yourself plunging into the void . . .

But now the scales have fallen from my eyes. I may have been an emotional cripple all my life, but suddenly I can walk, run, dance, sing and play the banjo. At least that's how I'm feeling after snorting a couple of preparatory lines, washed down with half a bottle of Krug.

We're meeting at Nah, a new club near Sloane Square started by a couple of 'It girls' who appear in all the right magazines but probably don't have two brain cells to rub together between them. It claims to offer the finest selection of vintage champagne served by the glass anywhere in London. Stupid idea. Why would anyone want vintage champagne by the glass?

From the outside it looks like a disused vehicle workshop with doormen out the front and a crowd of paparazzi hanging around. On the inside it looks like a disused vehicle workshop with a bar at one end and a DJ at the other on a raised platform. The music is so loud that I wonder what we'll actually be able to say to each other, but perhaps that's the idea. It was her choice. Everywhere I look there seem to be teenage girls in pussy-pelmet micro skirts and crop tops, with spiky hair and unhealthily pale skin – must be the effect of the light – and guys with earrings in torn jeans and muscle vests, also spiky haired and pale skinned. Have I come to the right place? I'm still wearing my suit, never thought to change; I don't think my skin's pale enough and I have no hair gel. I wouldn't normally care, but coming into this place makes me feel Jurassic.

I order a bottle of Cristal and two glasses, and place myself at a corner table overlooking the dance floor.

Two Livers keeps me waiting twenty minutes before appearing, wearing skintight leather pants, a white cotton off-the-shoulder blouse and bangles by Kiki. She's had her hair cut radically short and it makes her look even younger. She kisses me on the cheeks when she arrives and I capture the briefest hint of Un Bois Vanille by Serge

Lutens. I want to pull her to the floor and devour her, but this is not the place.

'You look fantastic. Champagne?' I have to raise my voice to be heard.

She nods and looks around. 'Crap location. Won't last. I give it three months.'

I nod back. There's not much we can do besides nodding and shouting the occasional remark, and we default to looking at the dancers and people-watching as the evening warms up and a few well-known faces appear.

Since we aren't really talking, I try to work out what we are doing. After a while I think I get it. We're hanging out. Just being together. The way we used to. Sometimes we'd talk endlessly, other times hardly at all. We didn't need to. Does it feel the same now? Not to me. I'm too nervous, sweating under my arms, my mouth a little too dry, and the champagne doesn't really help.

After a while she stands and pulls me up on to the dance floor. It's some techno number and I do my best to copy the kids but it really isn't me. She loses herself completely in a routine I've never seen her do before and it only makes me realise the distance that's grown between us.

When we get back to our seats she pulls me towards her. 'You weren't as bad as I thought.' And she plants a moist kiss on my lips, then gets up again before I can respond and heads to the powder room.

When she returns she looks as if she's done a couple of lines: her pupils are dilated and she has a slight delicious sheen of perspiration on her face – the sort I used to lick off her in the old days.

'Do you want to eat? I booked a couple of places just in case.'

She shakes her head. 'Let's dance again.'

It's not my sort of evening at all, but at least the second time we dance it's a slower number and I get the chance to put my arms around her and we can move together and I can inhale her scent. We end up back at our table with a second bottle, and then, because she really can drink for England, a third. I finally get it. We're hangin' and chillin' and seeing if the vibe is still there. After three bottles and quite a lot of coke, I think it is.

There's a commotion at the entrance. I can't hear what's going on because of the music, but I can see a group of huge men in suits with dark glasses talking to the doormen and pointing towards me. The doormen aren't small, but the new arrivals are a good head and shoulders taller.

Two Livers looks at them. 'What's going on over there? Who are those guys?'

'DLR Strummer. They're my lawyers.'

'Your lawyers? Are you serious? What are you doing?'

'We've done our first closing. I need everything ready for an investment committee tomorrow. My first.'

'Your first closing? So soon? Fantastic. How much did you raise?'

'Eighteen billion dollars.'

She looks at me, wide-eyed, amazed. 'Eighteen billion? Dave, no one raises eighteen billion for a first fund. You're lucky to raise anything.'

I shrug modestly. 'I have friends. I know a few people. I got lucky.'

She's eyeing me suspiciously. 'No one gets that lucky. Where did that money really come from?'

'Private banks, wealth managers, family offices, the usual.'

She's looking at me differently now, and I don't see this as positive. 'So what are you really doing?'

The lawyers are moving across the dance floor towards us, the dancers parting before them like waves before a battleship.

'What am I doing? Taking over the world. Well, the markets anyway. Global domination, starts tomorrow.'

I NEVER got to go back to her place. I knew I wouldn't. But I had to hope. When my legal team reached us with a stack of documents urgently requiring my signature, she used the opportunity to say goodnight, gave me the briefest of kisses on the cheek and went, turning heads and twisting a dagger in my heart.

I'm tired, lovesick but determined, and I have convened my first investment committee.

The office is different now. The traders have all gone, fired on very attractive terms and released from their period of notice so they can start work straight away with Mike Fisher to set up Caveman II somewhere around the corner. I'd have liked to have kept them, or some of them at any rate, but I can't have anyone on the inside that I can't trust totally. So I set them loose to start again. It'll take them months, maybe even a year, but I wish them well. I don't have that kind of time to play with.

In the meantime, I have a newly assembled elite team selected from among the friends and family of my backers. I insisted they all have some kind of relevant financial background, ideally that they'd trained at a major firm and knew what they were doing. In the end I got some technically competent people, but most of all I got people I can trust, all of whom are overseen by Maria, who sits in my outer office, probably wondering what on earth is going on but staying focussed by thinking about that million pound bonus at year end.

Around the table in my office I have the members of my investment committee. Carlos, inevitably, has to be there himself. Beside him, six others, ethnically diverse – we definitely tick the PC box big time – representing financial interests from China, the Middle East, Africa, Central and South America and Europe's Garlic Belt. They don't all look especially comfortable in suits and ties, and I'm not sure how great their understanding is of enterprise value or price earnings ratios, but their hearts – and wallets – are in the right place.

In a sense what we are going to do is the twenty-first century's answer to the buccaneers of the Elizabethan age. But whereas they set sail with cannons and cutlasses, we have computer screens and networks of trusted associates. We don't need violence. We just need money and brainpower. I guess it's progress.

I take my place at the end of the glass table, look around and clear my throat. I feel something's missing. Like a large, long-haired white cat sitting on my lap for me to stroke. Get a grip, Hart.

'Gentlemen, welcome to the inaugural investment committee of the Salvation Fund. The first item to note is that we completed our first closing on Tuesday with eighteen billion dollars in the bank. We have arranged dedicated credit lines to be secured against the holdings we acquire, which should allow us to take very much larger positions than just eighteen billion. And, of course, we'll be using derivatives and option strategies to maximise impact and achieve the greatest possible leverage.' I've tried to keep it simple but I can tell I've already lost most of them. 'With the support that should be available to us from . . . associated funds and investors, we should be able to move most markets. So, the world is our oyster. Where shall we go first?'

It takes an hour, and it's hardly the best informed discussion I've ever heard, but by the end we're all agreed. We reject Li Bing's proposal – short airline stocks and insurance companies and then start shooting down planes – and we turn down Pietro Valadoro's variation on it, doing the same thing but with cruise ships. I remind them that we're about investing for good and buying things, not selling them. And eventually, because I really can be quite persuasive, we get there.

I hit the button on the intercom.

'Maria – we'll need a smoker. I'm going on a business trip.'

I'VE BEEN to a dark place. Not a real one. A dark place in my mind. I was dreaming of all the lies I've told in my life. Well, not all of them. I couldn't possibly dream about all of them in a single night. And I don't mean the little lies that help to get you through life. 'Of course I'm not married.' 'I won't come in your mouth.' 'We don't need a condom. I had a vasectomy.' Just a few of the really big ones.

They say that communication is the sister of leadership, but I never tell anyone anything.

I certainly lied to Two Livers when I ran Grossbank. I told her I knew what I was doing. She was smart enough to know that no-one senior in investment banking really knows what they're doing. People at the top get by as best they can, hope for the best, and at year end look back on what's happened and call it their strategy. But when I said I knew what I was doing, I think she believed that I actually had a master plan. Because a lot of things did happen and they appeared to be intentional on my part and in the end they seemed to work out. Even though I rarely explained anything to her in advance, and a lot of the time was present in form only, having spent the previous night getting wrecked and lacking her constitution. But she showed faith in me. Faith that I didn't deserve. This particular emperor has never been anything other than stark naked.

So should I be pursuing her now? Am I worthy? If I care for her, shouldn't I just walk away before I fuck up again and hurt her, possibly destroy her?

Of course not. Idiot, Hart. Get a grip. I'm too selfish for that. And besides, she's a grown-up. She can look after herself. Probably better than I can.

Phew.

Better get some stronger pills.

I LOVE the Fatherland. Germany is a great country, with a great people and a great history. Okay, so from time to time they go a bit crazy and start invading small nations and all that shit, but we all have our off days.

I'm in Munich, city of beer, beautiful buildings and wonderful naked students sunbathing in the park they call the English Garden. Besides my lawyers from DLR Strummer, I have with me my new head of trading, a big black bodybuilder called Happy Mboku. Happy is from somewhere in West Africa. He found his way to Sierra Leone as a young man, made his name smuggling conflict diamonds and then decided on a career change when the Brits sent the Parachute Regiment to sort the place out. He ended up working in Antwerp for Rom Romanov, trading diamonds at least semi-legitimately, and acquired a financial education of sorts.

He looks short against the guys from DLR Strummer, but in fact he's six feet tall, weighs over two hundred and forty pounds and comfortably bench presses three times his own bodyweight. He could easily bench press me if he wanted. He doesn't really have a neck, just sprouts a head on top of very muscular, very broad shoulders. And he looks odd in a suit, even a bespoke Savile Row number that does its best to smooth over the bulges.

But the most interesting feature about Happy is the tribal markings on his face. When he reached puberty he was scarred – without anaesthetic – down both cheeks, in three straight lines on either side. He wasn't allowed to flinch or cry, because it was a rite of manhood. When the scars healed, they gave him the most ferocious appearance, which, combined with his natural tendency to frown, makes him the scariest man I've ever seen on a trading floor. He also has the widest smile, with perfect white teeth, which completely belies his normal appearance, but it is rarely seen.

We've come to visit yet another of those tired German family-run businesses that should never have had its shares listed on the stock exchange and is now paying the price, as perceived short-term under-performance over a couple of quarters is rewarded with an invasion of 'activist' shareholders and private-equity stalkers.

The company in question is called Meier Holding AG, and they're one of those old-fashioned outfits that still makes things. In this case everything from bathroom fittings to pumps to vehicle components and back again, via garden furniture, kitchen appliances and a stack of other items that really don't hang together and have no rhyme or reason, except the family that now only has a minority share in the business actually liked them – and still does. They're also old-fashioned in owning all their factories and land, not having any debt – the old man who founded the company didn't approve of it – and having never fired anyone except for just cause. Can you imagine? No employer provides jobs for life these days. But this company does, even if they don't disclose it, and they train their people, redeploy them between businesses if times are hard for one area while another is doing well, and have a paternalistic attitude straight out of the nineteenth century. They also have an outstanding labour record, with no strikes, minimal absenteeism and high productivity. But who cares about that these days?

Clearly a business like this has a massive target on its back, and it hasn't taken a genius at some investment bank or other to notice it and come up with a plan. The thing that corporate financiers have in common with hedge fund managers is that they are morally neutral. If, on the one hand, they could raise finance for a company, help it expand, make acquisitions, develop new products and create jobs and prosperity for the future, or, on the other hand, mount a hostile bid for it, sell off the most valuable parts of the business, asset-strip it, load it with debt and fire half the workforce, leaving it terminally ill, they'll always be consistent. They'll do whatever makes the biggest fees.

In the case of Meier Holding, an analyst working an all-nighter in the slave-labour camp known as the 'associates pool' at Hardman Stoney decided the biggest fee-earning potential lay in taking this company down. He (or conceivably she) would never have visited the company or met the management, let alone the workforce. It would have been a numbers-based decision. Everything in life comes down to numbers in the end.

So now the Meier family have the Terminator Fund out of Chicago on their shareholder register. Terminator is a hostile 'activist' hedge fund that boasts of its ability to 'shake up' management in the interests of maximising shareholder value. They were started by some ex-Schleppenheim M & A bankers who lost their jobs when the firm went bust in the crisis and bounced back with their own outfit. In this case they've teamed up with a private equity firm called Night Fury LLP, named after a mythical fire-breathing dragon in a children's film that never missed its target.

Well, maybe they never missed before. But that was before the good guys arrived. Or maybe I should say 'the bad guys'. But aren't *they* the bad guys? And if they're the bad guys, who are we? We're the even worse guys. Whatever.

We head off to the company's headquarters in a couple of rented limos and pull up outside what are surprisingly pretty modest offices. I have a proposal to put to their board, which is having a last-minute meeting before going into an extraordinary general meeting of shareholders called by the activists who want to unlock all that wonderful value.

THE THING about shareholder meetings is that while you can prepare endlessly for them, rehearsing, brainstorming, war-gaming, doing dry runs in front of a 'red team' prepped to give you a hard time, you can never predict exactly what will happen.

So Guy Marshall from the Terminator Fund, a preppy, twenty-eight-year-old American with an MBA from Chicago Business School and enough arrogance for a whole auditorium full of people, looks around the conference room in the Hotel Plaza with quite a lot of disdain. It's full of little people, ordinary shareholders, many of them retired employees of Meier Holding, local businessmen and professionals, a few institutional fund managers, but only one face he recognises. Matt Warner from Night Fury is also there. His frat buddy and fellow Chicago MBA. They are dressed alike, look alike, talk the same way, think the same things, have the same haircut, belong to the same club, probably married the same woman and will eventually have identical children. And they are members of the global elite who hover above the lesser masses and determine their fate.

Except that above them today hovers someone else. Me. Oh, and Happy Mboku's here too.

I'm waiting for little Guy to go to the men's room. He has to before the meeting starts, because there's no telling how long it will last – an awful lot of these little people might want to have their say about the fate of 'their' company – or when the key votes will take place, and he can't afford to miss one. Eventually, he looks at his watch – we have about five minutes to go – leaves his papers on his chair to secure his seat and heads towards the men's room. Happy leaves his own papers on the chair directly behind Guy's, and then he and I tuck in behind our target.

When he enters the gents we follow. There are two other men in there already and we wait until they leave, pretending to wash our hands while Guy is at the urinals. Then Happy places a No Entry sign on the outside of the door and I approach Guy just as he's standing at the washbasin.

'I don't believe we've met?'

He looks up and immediately recognises me. That's the power of the press.

'You're Dave Hart. Everyone knows you. Mr Hart – a pleasure, sir.'

He dries his hands and steps forward as if to shake and formally introduce himself.

'No need. I know you already.'

'You . . . know me?'

My face is deadpan. I give no indication of any feelings or emotion, although I have a scar on my forehead where he can see a pulse racing.

'That's right. And so does my associate.'

His eyes flicker towards the huge black man blocking the door. Happy is letting his face relax nicely into a frown.

'This is Happy. Happy Mboku. He's head of trading at my new fund.'

Happy inclines his head obligingly.

'Your . . . head of trading?'

'He also trades. Guy . . . may I call you Guy?'

He nods nervously.

'Guy, you and I find ourselves on opposite sides of the table today.'

'Opposite sides?' His voice sounds a little squeaky.

'That's right.' I put my hand on his shoulder and lean closer to him. 'And that's a huge shame.'

'W-why is that?'

Happy has left his station by the door to stand behind Guy and, with an instinctive touch, leans forward, places powerful hands on either side of his neck and starts to massage him. Guy flinches and glances back at him.

'D-do you mind?'

'Not at all.' Happy's voice is a deep bass growl. I'd love to hear him do 'Old Man River'. He carries on massaging.

'Mr Hart, what is going on here? What are you actually doing?'

'Guy, I'm trying to be persuasive. For your own sake. I'm trying to persuade you to change your mind on voting out the management of Meier Holding – my friends – and to pack up your things and go home to Chicago.'

'W-what are you talking about? I'm here representing the firm. We've made our position clear. This is business.'

'Ah yes, business. I remember business.' A long pause as I look wistfully around the room. 'Guy, did you hear that I died?'

'Everyone did, Mr Hart.'

'That's right, Guy. But then I came back. And since I came back, I'm . . . different. I used to believe in the power of persuasion. Now I just believe in . . . power.'

Right on cue, Happy ups the pressure on Guy's neck.

'W-what are you doing?'

'I'm telling you – not asking – *telling* you what you're going to do this afternoon.'

'W-what's that?'

I drop my voice so that I'm almost whispering, and he has to strain to hear me.

'Listen carefully. You're going to go back to your seat, sit down and reflect on just how much you enjoy your life at –' I get a piece of paper from my jacket pocket and glance at it – 'at Lincoln Park Avenue, in your swanky condo overlooking the park and with that amazing view towards Lake Michigan, with Lillian and your dog Skipper and, if nothing happens to you, your first child. Perhaps you'll have a son. That would be just grand, wouldn't it, Guy? Guy Junior. Imagine those proud grandparents.' I refer to the paper again. 'Imagine Doug and Lucy and how proud they'll be of their little girl's first child. And your mom and pop too. George and Hannah. There's so much love surrounding you, Guy. So much that's positive. So let's not spoil things. You go on back to your seat. And once you've had a chance to reflect on all the things I've told you, you're going to decide it's a bad idea to vote the way you were thinking. Then we'll be on the same side. You want to be on the same side as me, don't you, Guy?'

'Mr Hart . . . I . . . I have instructions. I could be fired.'

'You could. But there are worse things, Guy. Trust me. There are worse things.'

He's gone very pale and says nothing, just nods.

Happy releases him and he straightens his jacket and tries to regain his dignity as he heads for the door. Just before he leaves, I call after him.

'Oh, Guy – I'm sitting at the back. You'll see me with my legal team. But Happy . . . he'll be sitting behind you. Right behind you.'

IT'S THREE hours later and the Sekt is flowing. If there is a God, I never worked out why he gave the French champagne and the Germans Sekt. Maybe it's all those small countries they invaded. Whatever the reason, Happy and I are drinking it, along with the board of Meier Holding and their friends and supporters.

Fritz Meier, the elderly, straight-backed, patrician son of the founder, and chair of the supervisory board, slaps me on the back for about the fifth time and shakes his head.

'This is the happiest day for me, Mr Hart. The day we thought we would lose the company has turned into the day we secured its future. And the Americans – those Terminators – they did nothing. Amazing. We watched him. We waited for him to raise his hand. He just sat there.'

'Yes, it was amazing, wasn't it? I think the other American, the one from Night Fury, lived up to his name in the end. He looked as if he was taken by surprise that his associate didn't say anything. They had a plan. They were meant to be in this together. He was mad as hell.'

'They had a fight at the end. Outside. The two of them were shouting and pushing each other.'

'Really? That's too bad. Some people don't know how to behave.'

'I think he was ill.'

'Which one?'

'The one from the Terminator Fund. The one your colleague, Herr Mboku, sat behind. His face was white like paper. Perhaps your colleague's presence put him off?'

'Happy put someone off? Never.'

We all laugh. Then he turns serious.

'Mr Hart, your investment proposal from your new fund has saved our company. We are very grateful.'

It's true. The legal team are working on it while we're drinking pretend champagne. Salvation is investing two hundred million Euros in Meier Holding in a friendly deal at a discounted price, on the understanding that they don't change their strategy or practices at all and just keep on doing what they were doing already. Around the world, a dozen other similar companies are sitting down with teams from DLR Strummer, who are laying out proposals on our behalf. I always say, if in doubt, go large.

Fritz taps a spoon against an empty champagne glass to get everyone's attention. 'Ladies and gentlemen, I propose a toast. To the Salvation Fund, its founder, Mr Dave Hart, and his friends and associates.'

They all raise their glasses and toast Columbian drug barons, Italian Mafiosi, the Triads, the Yakuza and all the rest. Though of those present only Happy and I know whose health we are really drinking.

What Fritz also doesn't know is that the Silver Fox has orchestrated the biggest press coverage this company has ever received.

Meier Holding is a conglomerate, a grouping of diverse businesses across a range of industries. They have strength in depth but, more importantly, breadth, as they span so many areas of activity. And in troubled times that makes them both robust in adversity, because they spread risk, and well placed to bounce back with the economy when the upturn comes. At least that's the story in tomorrow's papers as every quoted conglomerate in the German, and every other major market, gets caught in a feeding frenzy of buyers. The Salvation Fund will lead the charge, naturally, with friends from low places hot on our heels and the rest of the market, caught out by the sudden change of sentiment, scrambling to catch up. Tomorrow will be a good day for conglomerates all around the world. They're back in fashion. And even better for those of us who quietly accumulated holdings in those same companies ahead of today's events.

THERE WAS one footnote, right at the end, that's worth recording. Happy was half pissed, having consumed more than his own bodyweight in Sekt, and pulled me to one side, where no one could hear us.

'Mr Hart, sir.'

'Dave. Happy, you can call me Dave.'

He shakes his head. 'Doesn't feel right, sir. Mr Romanov, he likes to be called Mr Romanov.'

'That's fine, Happy, but you're on my team now.'

'Dave . . . sir. I want you to know how much I enjoyed today.'

'Good. I'm pleased to hear that, Happy.'

'No, sir, I mean I *really* enjoyed it. I'd like to do it again.'

'Why?'

'It's the people, sir. Look around. They're good people. Decent people. And they're really pleased. We made a big difference today.'

'I guess that's right, Happy.'

He looks around the room, beaming at everyone with his big, wide grin. 'And we didn't even have to kill anyone.'

WHEN A man has a major triumph, he naturally wants to celebrate. Celebration might take many forms – and I tend to like all of them – but in this particular case all I can think of is that I want to see the woman I'm convinced is the love of my life. So we head to the airport and I call Two Livers.

Frustratingly, her office says she's not available. I try her mobile, but it goes straight to voicemail.

'It's me. I've had a great day. Really great. I'd love to tell you all about it. And I'm definitely in the mood to celebrate. I'm in the Fatherland, smoking into Biggin Hill around 6.30. If you're free tonight, let me take you out. Anywhere you want.'

When I hang up, I realise I sounded like a kid, over-excited, immature, jumping up and down for his parents' attention. But why hide things from her? This is me. I want her to know me. On second thoughts, she knows me pretty well already, which is a troubling thought. Would anyone who really knows me ever be seriously interested in me? We reach the airport and I drown the thought in a bottle of proper champagne.

She doesn't call, so I try her again when we land, and again when I get to the Ritz, but without success. Damn. I'm on a high and want to do something, but I'm by myself. Once upon a time that wouldn't have mattered. As a young investment banker in London, well heeled and searching for stimulation, I'd have contacted a few escort agencies – the kind you find these days on the internet – chosen a girl or two according to my taste, and who I'd had lately, and arranged some gratifyingly meaningless sex, probably enhanced by drugs and definitely by booze. And afterwards, they'd have left, with no comebacks or consequences, keeping everything neat, clean and simple. That, by the way, is what you pay for with professionals. You're not paying for sex. You're paying for them to leave afterwards. It's the ones you don't pay for who hang around and complicate your life. Those you pay for later.

Further on in my career, when I was more successful and more demanding, I kept a private list of more exclusive, high-end girls not available to the internet-surfing public, and called them up for equally meaningless but much more expensive sex, definitely with drugs – which they could supply – and very fine booze.

But now that I'm in love, that all seems so yesterday. I want a meaningful relationship now. I've reached a turning point in my life and there's no looking back. I want commitment.

That feeling lasts almost half an hour.

In the end, feeling lonely and rather empty, I call one of the girls I used to see – Giselle, from Brazil – not for sex, just for companionship and the snappy, quick-witted banter that I used to enjoy with her.

'Dave – how are you, honey?' She sounds half asleep. 'I thought you were dead.'

I hate 'honey'. She might as well call me 'sweetie-pie'.

'I'm good, babe. I was dead, but I came back.' Why do I call her 'babe'? No idea, I just seem to go into another mode. Perhaps it's a two-way thing. Honey meets babe.

'Uhhh . . . yeah . . . I think I heard something about that.'

I know. She sounds doped out. Too many late nights, too many drugs. But I had her number and I need some company.

Luckily, she's not doing anything tonight, so we agree to meet at Mimi's. I shower and change and find I'm quite looking forward to seeing her again.

PHYSICALLY, GISELLE is a sex bomb. Five foot six, dark, dusky skin, long hair, size eight but totally pneumatic, she'd turn heads if she were dressed as a nun. But she isn't. She's wearing a bra-less halter top that leaves nothing to the imagination, with long white pants so tight that if she wasn't shaved between the legs you could count her pubic hairs. I'm hanging around outside Mimi's, and when she gets out of her cab she looks like exactly what she is: a thousand pounds a night of paid-for sex, offering OWO (oral sex without a condom), CIM (you can come in her mouth) and A-plus (anal sex as an extra, depending on your size). I think it was a US president who once said he didn't feel he knew a woman until he'd had her three different ways. Generally I don't go down that particular route – happy to leave back doors to politicians. Quite what inspires stunningly beautiful girls to come to London from all over the world, leaving the places they grew up in, missing their loved ones and lying down – or standing up, or kneeling – to satisfy guys like me is beyond me. It might be lucrative, but it can't be fun.

But as long as they do, I'm up for it.

She squeals with mock delight and rushes forward and throws her arms around . . . a guy behind me with wavy grey hair, a beer belly and a double chin. He's leaving the club with a woman I presume is his wife – she's just about attractive enough, but not enough to earn a living on the internet – and I find the two of them pretty weird. Who takes their wife to a nightclub? Are they trying to convince people they drink and dance and have fun together, despite being married? Anyway, Giselle presses herself against him, he looks baffled, his wife looks furious and I try not to laugh.

'Giselle! I'm here. It's Dave. Here I am.'

Brain of Brazil looks puzzled, disentangles herself from the guy with the belly and the chin, and squeals even louder and throws her arms around me.

We head inside and I approach the maître d', who spots some crumpled notes in my hand and comes over so that I can slip them to him. He then obligingly finds us a table beside the dance floor. A magnum of Cristal appears at our table unbidden – it's understood that it goes with the territory if you want the best spot – and I call over a waiter and order a magnum of U'Luvka vodka as well, with a tray of mixers and a bucket of ice. We won't finish either, in fact we may hardly touch them, but spending this much will ensure not only that we're left alone, but if we choose to misbehave – let's say I direct Giselle discreetly under the table – no one will take offence.

Giselle seems to be having trouble speaking, and I wonder if she took something before she came out. Did she feel she needed to in order to get through the evening? Maybe. It has to take a toll. What these girls do is worse than investment banking. We might have to grease up, bend over, grasp our ankles and say stick it in and make it hurt – but it only happens metaphorically, with clients and bosses and board members, and we get paid millions for it. A thousand pounds a night doesn't really cut it for me.

Since she's finding it hard to talk, and is obviously aware of the problem, she opts for a better tactic and pulls me up onto the dance floor. The pulsating lights, the noise and the relative anonymity of the semi-darkness usually ensure that I can dance with my date unnoticed by anyone else who might be there. But tonight Giselle throws herself into a routine she could only have learnt in a lap-dancing bar in Rio. She gyrates, spins, turns, runs her hands up and down first her body then mine – stopping nowhere – and by the end every head in the place has turned our way. Bring on the cabaret. I feel like I'm part of a floor show. Eventually the number comes to an end and I drag her back to the table.

Which is when I see we're not alone. Another couple have placed themselves at our table and are helping themselves to our champagne.

I'm about to get very aggressive – so aggressive, in fact, that I might actually call a waiter over – when I recognise the man. It's Vladimir Kommisarov, who runs First Siberian

Bank in London. He's early forties, fair-haired, tall and good-looking. OneSib, as his firm is known, is one of the biggest Russian banks, and he heads their London investment banking operations. Their traders are famously punchy and aggressive, and are known as the Red Army Trading Team. When he first arrived in London, I saw in Vlad someone potentially interesting – a kindred spirit – and helped him. Now that I'm back from the dead, Vlad the Impaler – named for his prowess with women, rather than anything more sinister – has spotted me and decided to make his number.

'Dave – welcome back. How was it on the other side?'

'Vlad, good to see you. The other side?'

He turns to the lady with him – whom I find hard to place, because she's a little old to be working, but looks ravishing in a Roberto Cavalli three-quarter-length dress, gathered at the side to show off her figure, and a Bulgari cocktail necklace with coloured gemstones that pick out the colours in the dress. She's the complete package, stylish and sexy, and I decide she's definitely edible.

'My darling – this is Dave Hart. We saw him on the television. He used to run Grossbank. He was very successful and then . . . he died and came back to life again!' He says this with a big grin. 'Dave, this is my wife, Anya.'

His wife? Fuck. Another guy who takes his wife out in the evening to have a good time. So why does he play around so much? Because he can? Because it's there? Because he's too like me?

'A pleasure to meet you, Mr Hart.' Anya has a deliciously husky voice and a strong Russian accent. I could eat her for her voice alone, but it gets better. We shake hands and she has a bone-crunching grip. Wow.

I suddenly feel inadequate having only Giselle to introduce. Where is Two Livers?

'Call me Dave.' I turn to my companion. 'This is my friend Giselle from Brazil. Giselle – let me introduce Anya and Vlad.'

Anya sees through her instantly. 'Of course. We saw you dancing.'

'I liked your dancing.' Vlad's trying to pay her a compliment, but it draws a dagger-like glance from Anya. 'But, my darling, Giselle dances very well.' Stop digging, Vlad.

Giselle tries to say something but she still can't and looks as if her eyes are slightly out of control, rolling upwards when she isn't concentrating. She's perspiring too, and seems unsteady on her feet. Probably put too much into the dancing. We sit down and a waiter appears and pours us all more drinks. I'd normally expect to catch up with Vlad on business while the ladies talk shopping. Only Giselle can't talk.

'So, Dave, I've heard a lot about this fund you've raised. Eighteen billion, is that right? It's huge. Where did it all come from?'

I grin at him. He knows full well where part of it comes from. 'Well, some of it's Russian, Vlad.'

'I thought so. Russians are good investors for people who think big. We understand large ventures with big ambitions.'

On my left, I'm vaguely aware of Giselle, who seems to be staring at someone at the next table. I look across and can see two black men, both with shaven heads and earrings, wearing what look like Armani suits and shoes with no socks. Did no one tell them the *Miami Vice* look is out? They have one 'lady' sitting with them, and she looks as if she's Giselle's twin sister. What's wrong with these guys? Are they planning a reverse threesome? Surely they need at least one girl each?

One of the men catches my eye and says something to the other, and now they're both glaring at me with obvious hostility, when Giselle suddenly picks up her champagne glass and throws the contents over the girl. The victim is stunned, looks down at her see-through top, which I'd say has just got a whole lot better courtesy of a fine glass of Cristal, and then grabs a glass from their table and throws it back, missing Giselle but drenching Anya. Everyone stands up and I find myself stepping aside as Giselle, ridiculously, throws a whole ice bucket over the three of them. And then I don't step aside and get soaked with the contents of their ice bucket. Vlad tries to shield Anya from further damage and, for his trouble, gets a glass of red wine down his jacket.

Finally, Giselle manages to speak.

'Whore!' she cries at the girl at the other table.

'You can talk, bitch!' she screams back.

This is quite exciting. I want to yell 'Catfight!' but think better of it. I realise we're attracting a lot of attention and can see the club doormen heading fast in our direction. I turn to Giselle.

'Don't tell me, you two know each other.'

'W-we worked together. Whore ripped me off.'

'Bitch ripped me off,' comes the screamed reply.

Then a fist connects with my jaw. One of the black guys has stepped forward and taken a swing at me, sending me sprawling across the table, knocking over bottles and glasses. Giselle sways in my direction. I think she's going to help me get up, which I'm not sure is a good idea – I'd rather stay down – and then she throws up all over me. Which is probably fortunate, because the black guy has come forward to finish me off, and instead steps back to avoid getting splashed with vomit. It stinks, and my shirt is soaked and sticks to me, and some of it even went on my face, so I almost feel like throwing up myself. Anya and Vlad have leapt back to try to avoid getting splashed, but too late. It's a fucking mess, and the black guys still want to settle it physically.

It's then that the cavalry, in the form of the doormen, arrive at our table. There are eight of them – where did they all come from? – and they take a firm grip on our arms, walk us to the bar, where they demand that we settle our bills, and then take us outside. I'm not even allowed a diversion via the men's room to clean up.

It's only then that the flashbulbs start popping – there's a no-paparazzi rule inside the club – and people start getting excited. I expect to hear my name being called, but instead they're shouting about the D Boyz. Who are they talking about? Evidently the black guys, who are clearly much more famous than Dave Hart. They're shown to a limo with the girl who double-crossed Giselle and, as they get in, one of them turns and makes a gun with his hand and pretends to shoot me. Then he draws his finger across his throat and grins, but not in a nice way, and mouths some words. I can't be sure, but it's something like, 'You're dead, motherfucker'. Can you believe this? He's threatening me. On top of everything else that's happened this evening, this man is threatening me. Is he serious? Is he really planning to come after me? It wouldn't be hard to work out who I am, or where I can be found. I don't like threats, especially serious ones. I really don't like them.

So I'm left apologising to Vlad and Anya, while Giselle, whose front is also soaked in vomit, leans against me, her eyes rolling upwards into their sockets. The stench alone is enough to make me heave. What was she eating? If I stare long enough at my front, I could probably work it out.

Vlad thinks the whole thing is a scream. 'Dave, you are amazing. Wherever you go, things happen. It's great.'

Anya evidently doesn't share his enthusiasm for being amazed. She stares resolutely away and then their car arrives and they too disappear. One of the doormen looks at me with sympathy. 'Cab?'

'Two.'

He whistles and a black cab pulls up. I open the door and ignore the driver's hostile stare.

'If you two are getting in here in that state, it'll be an extra forty quid.'

'It's just her.' I peel off a couple of fifties and pass them through the window.

Giselle can barely stand and I help her onto the back seat and strap her in.

'Dave . . .'

'What is it, Giselle?'

'Dave . . . don't you want to have sex with me?'

'Not tonight, Giselle. I'll call you.'

'Dave . . .'

'What?'

'Dave . . . my money.'

I look down at my vomit-stained front and put my hand to the side of my face, which is aching and starting to swell. 'Are you serious?'

'It's a thousand . . . for the night.'

And because I'm a man, and once again I'm weak, I

stand by the open door of the cab and peel off more notes and hand them in to her, trying not to catch the eye of the driver in his rear-view mirror.

I've had better celebrations.

IT GETS worse the next day.

My right eye has swollen almost shut and when I prise it open the white of my eye is almost completely red with burst blood vessels. A blue-green bruise covers most of my upper cheek. I took a hell of a punch to the side of my face and I'm lucky nothing's broken.

My suit's ruined, and my shirt, but who cares? The real damage is in the newspapers.

Apparently the D Boyz are US rap artists touring the UK with their latest album. People outside the insulated world of investment banking have heard of these guys, are interested in them, and of course, the papers will pay for their pictures when they get into trouble. Which is why there's a photo of me, covered in vomit and propping up a clearly spaced-out Giselle, in almost every newspaper.

Shit. Maybe Two Livers is abroad. Perhaps she won't read the papers today. Maybe she'll think it was another guy called Dave Hart.

And then I check my voicemail and it goes from bad to very bad indeed. She was tied up in a board meeting most of the day and well into the evening, but left a message around nine saying she'd love to meet, and how about having a late supper at Wild Honey, a Michelin one-star restaurant in Mayfair. It's fully booked, but she's called in a favour and got us a table, and if she doesn't hear back from me will meet me there. Damn.

What to do? If all else fails, tell the truth. I wanted to

see you but couldn't get hold of you. So I waited half an hour, then called a Brazilian hooker instead, and she was out of her mind on drugs and puked on me and caused a fight and I got thumped and thrown out of the club and that's why my face is in the papers. Oh and, by the way, some rapper is threatening to kill me. I know I'm sad, and I feel like a total loser. I'd rather have been with you, and I really am committed to our relationship and seeing if we can make things work. Honestly.

Would she believe me? Maybe not.

MARIA AND Tom are sitting in the outer office, looking out at the trading floor. Tom will be driving me to my next meeting and has come up for a coffee and a chat with Maria. No doubt he wants to take the temperature of how I'm feeling. He's read the papers.

My door's open and I tune into their conversation while I pretend to stare at something on one of the screens on my desk.

Maria is talking. She's very kindly removed all the newspapers from the office and binned them. My black eye is reminder enough of a less than successful evening. What pleases me more is that the conversation isn't just about me messing up again.

'. . . the fund's up half a billion Euros!'

'Half a billion?' Tom sounds impressed.

'On paper, of course.'

'Of course.' Our conglomerates play has worked out so far.

Tom looks out at the trading floor. Happy Mboku is waving his arms around and shouting down the phone, stamping his feet and looking as if he might injure someone.

'What's that one doing?'

'He's ordering lunch. They have deliveries every day.'

'Funny bunch, aren't they?'

It's true. From time to time in the City, a trader is found to be a criminal. He breaks the rules, deals on inside information or ahead of a client order, or in some other way falls foul of the law. Occasionally he even gets prosecuted. But nowhere is there a firm that only employs criminals. Fortunately, for the authorisation of this firm by the Financial Services Authority, none of them has a criminal record in any jurisdiction that shares information with the Brits.

Sitting next to Happy is Nobukatsu Yokoyama from Osaka. Nob was training to be a sumo wrestler – he's six foot five and weighs thirty-two stone – but took a pay-off early on from the wrong guys, got kicked out of school and ended up working for the Yakuza. I'm told his body is covered in tattoos, though I didn't bother to check in the job interview. His left hand is missing the pinkie – apparently another Yakuza idiosyncrasy. Fuck with me and I'll cut your pinkie off – or better yet, make you cut it off yourself. Strange lot, the Japanese. Nob is here on behalf of Bang Bang Lee. I thought the Triads and the Yakuza didn't get on, but it turns out there are eight hundred thousand Chinese living in Japan, and most of them are online gaming clients of Bang Bang's. So he has business in Japan and trusted lieutenants to look after his interests there. Nob has only limited English, which is one reason why we can call him Nob.

We also have Sly, from Miami, representing the US East Coast syndicate, a tall, lean Latino panther of a man who never rushes anything and always looks as if he's working out how best to kill you before he answers a question. Sly has a scar running down one side of his face from his hairline to his chin, via his eye – which is covered by a black eye patch. Apparently his right eye socket is empty, though again I never felt the need to check during the job interview. Timur is from Kazakhstan, a former Kazakh wrestler with a shaved head and a pony tail, who looks like he just rode into town with Genghis Khan, and there are a bunch of others of equally impressive parentage. I look at them with pride. My team. My boys. My dirty dozen.

'Tom – let's go.' I take my jacket from the back of my chair and straighten my tie. Normally I don't wear one. In 'hedge fund alley' around St James's, the uniform for the rich and successful, as well as for those who want to look as if they're rich and successful, is a serious business suit, crisp white shirt, but open neck – and a tie in the desk drawer in case you need it.

But today I'm going to the Treasury. Her Majesty's Treasury in Whitehall, and I want to look the part. There was a time when hedge funds, country funds and emerging markets funds used to buy up the debt of smaller countries, or pick up assets cheaply in those same countries, and joked about buying the places. Today I'm going to see if I can buy a chunk of Britain. The way I see it, after all this country's been through, it's a bargain, and there's no harm in trying.

The Treasury building had a revamp a few years ago and went from being impressive on the outside and impractical on the inside, to still being impressive on the outside but with a large dose of tacky modern 'style' on the inside – including a cafeteria where senior mandarins can go to fetch their own coffee, this being an egalitarian age – and, of course, it remains impractical.

You enter the building through airport-style security, manned by what I guess are minimum wage job-creation victims who'd rather be on the dole and whose motivation and attention to detail achieve the same high levels as their counterparts at Heathrow. But it's only the Treasury, afterall.

I've arranged to meet my legal team there and asked them to send someone via Café Nero and load up with trays of coffee. We enter the building like a visiting delegation, and you can see the people in the entrance looking and wondering who the visiting politician is with the secret service bodyguard.

The senior civil servant present is a pugnacious, grey-haired man with a Village People moustache.

'Mr Hart, good morning and welcome. Do sit down. I'm afraid I can't offer you anything to drink.'

I glance at my watch. It's 10 a.m. 'No problem. It's pretty rare that I drink at this time of day.'

He smiles wanly. 'I meant tea or coffee, Mr Hart. It's the austerity measures. Tap water?'

'Never touch it. But we've arranged our own coffee.'

On cue, there's a discreet knock at the door and the two last members of our team, junior lawyers, arrive with trays of coffee. Treasury civil servants being sharper than most, they look at the trays and gratifying looks of relief spread across their faces as they realise we've brought enough for them as well.

Civil servants are used to humiliation, but even they find it infra dig to start meetings by apologising that due to the austerity measures they can't offer their visitors tea or coffee. So today is a bonanza. A well-prepared visitor – briefed by the Silver Fox – has done a coffee run. What bliss. One of them steps outside and I hear a whispered conversation, and then I'm told that the minister is coming too. Nothing to do with the large café latte going spare at the end of the table, I'm sure. Once Britain controlled the finances of the Empire from this building. Cash for access? How about coffee?

The civil servants are clearly in awe of my legal advisers. I've brought six of them, including the coffee team, and they sit on either side of me. It's good, because it diverts attention from my black eye. At least I think it does. I really don't need six lawyers with me, and it's a silly indulgence, but if you're going into someone else's territory, you might as well be fully armed. So the Treasury team are outnumbered and outgunned on their own turf. Nice. I like to feel in charge on other people's turf. Probably comes from me being short, like Hitler and Napoleon.

I still haven't introduced them, and their appearance is quite intimidating, so Village People takes me to one side and whispers, 'Mr Hart – who are these people?'

'My lawyers. DLR Strummer. They're huge.'

'I can see they're huge.'

'No. They're a huge law firm. Biggest in the world.'

'Oh. Why are they here? Why so many?' He looks at the tall, dark-suited, heavily built men in dark glasses, sitting at the conference table, setting up laptops and unloading briefcases of paperwork, and I can see he's sceptical.

I pat him on the back. 'Relax. They may be lawyers, but they also do coffee. Very handy if the meeting overruns.'

'They fetch your coffee? You mean they'd go for more?'

'If I ask nicely.'

The minister who joins us isn't a real minister at all. He's a friend of the party, suddenly elevated to the peerage after the election and given ministerial office to bring to bear the benefit of his business expertise for the sake of the government. I have mixed feelings about this. Jobs (and peerages) for the boys without the inconvenience of exposure to the electorate, who get to pick up the tab, doesn't seem quite right in the twenty-first century. On the other hand, we need people in government who actually understand how things work in the real world. We can't get by just with MPs who can handle a mean garden fete or play cards in the local working men's club, or, worse still, professional politicians who have only ever worked in Central Office since leaving university and wouldn't have a prayer of holding down a real job without a team of advisers to delegate it to.

So when Lord Bigmann comes in I stand along with everyone else, incline my head, smile nicely when we shake hands and call him 'my lord', which rather takes him and everyone else by surprise, because they know I don't mean it. In return he tries not to stare at my black eye.

Lord Bigmann was a scrap-metal merchant, which is handy because now he advises the chancellor on how to handle our currency. He's also rather pleased with himself in an overweight, huffing-and-puffing but still energetic kind of way and, as a gritty northern lad of humble stock, he is obviously delighted to be a member of the best club in London, the House of Lords, with excellent parking facilities and a very convivial bar.

'So, Mr Hart, we've all read a lot about you in recent times, and seen you on the telly. Quite a celebrity. What can we do for you?'

'Thank you, my lord. You're very kind. But I'm hoping I can do something for you. For the country, really. With my new fund.'

'The Salvation Fund? Britain certainly needs salvation. Don't quote me on that.'

I glance at my lawyers. 'Anything said within these four walls today is entirely confidential, my lord. Strictly between ourselves.'

Yeah, right. Us and our three hundred closest friends and associates.

'My lord, my fund was created to make positive, supportive investments. We provide long-term, patient capital to help build for the future. We call it "investing for good". And we want to back Britain.'

He chuckles. 'Wonderful, Mr Hart, but what does that mean?'

'It means we're in the market to invest in state entities, to buy assets that don't need to remain in state hands, and provide the financial commitment for the future which is needed but which the government can't currently undertake itself because of the austerity measures.'

'Mr Hart, you have form in this area. You once offered to buy the NHS.'

Bastard.

But it's true. It was one of those foolish things that we're all guilty of at some point in our lives. I was pissed, it was the early hours of the morning, I was leaving a night club and heading back to the apartment for, I think, a threesome, and was confronted by some press people. They wanted a quote about some bullshit or other that I wasn't ready to talk about, so I said the first thing that came into my head. Well, you do, don't you? In this case, I said I thought Grossbank should buy the NHS. We'd streamline it, run it properly, empower the front-line medical staff and fire the medicrats, put some commercial discipline into the organisation – and we'd all be winners. Especially Grossbank. It seemed a good idea at the time, the way lots of things do at two in the morning when you're pissed.

'My lord, we're in a very different investment climate now. The proposals we've brought today are focussed, specific ideas that will help Britain get back on its feet. We're prepared to stand by them and back them with our own money.' And it's not two in the morning and I'm not pissed. Yet.

'Go on.'

Christ, he sounds like me. Looks like me too, poker-faced, glancing occasionally to either side of me to check what my lawyers are doing. I told them to bring other work along, because there wouldn't be anything for them to do here other than look good, so they are writing, typing into laptops, taking notes and tapping into their Blackberries. Unfortunately, this has spooked the civil service team, who are furiously writing down everything we say, clearly concerned in case the away team have better records than the minister.

'We have three ideas. Big ideas. I'll outline them in concept and then, if you're interested, we would propose to come back and make a formal presentation with the detail of what we have in mind.'

'So you've come here to fly some kites? All right. Go on.'

Fucking scrap-metal merchant.

'My lord, I'll be brief . . .'

'Good.'

Now I'm getting mad. He only came for the coffee.

'First, real estate. The government – the Crown – owns an awful lot of buildings, land, roads –'

'Yes, yes, I know what we own. Go on.'

'We would propose to transfer ownership of all those assets into a holding company – we've called it UKRealCo – in which the Salvation Fund and some of our associated investors would make a significant investment – real money, my lord. Tens of billions. We'd use that money to help finance not only ongoing repairs and maintenance but also the development and modernisation of the estate. Then, at an opportune moment when markets have recovered and sentiment is better, we float it on the stockmarket in a mammoth privatisation-type share issue. It would be one of the biggest and most powerful real-estate companies in the world. It would get all the ongoing obligations of the portfolio off the state's balance sheet and into the private sector. And, of course, we would offer voters – I mean, the public – the chance to buy shares in the company at the flotation price. It would be a major strategic event for UK plc and nothing like it has ever been done before.'

He sits back at this point and scratches his chin. 'So we put everything into this company, all of our property assets, you and your mates buy in at an attractive price, it gets floated on the stockmarket at a higher price and the public, who already owned it in the first place, get the chance to buy it again?'

I'm going to have to rethink my view of scrap-metal merchants. 'My lord, it's a matter of presentation.'

'Most things are, Mr Hart.' He glances at his watch. 'What's your next idea?'

Some days even my awesomeness has its limitations. I do need a drink, after all.

'Our second idea is the environment.'

'The environment?'

'And natural resources. The two go hand in hand. The

careful and sympathetic development of those limited remaining assets that nature has bequeathed to this country.' Bequeathed? Where did I get that one? 'We'd like to buy an option to develop any natural resources found in the UK, both onshore and offshore, from a specified list of items – items which are mostly low profile and not politically sensitive. Shale gas, for example, which turns out to be pretty commonly found in a bunch of places, rare earths, which we think might be found in very low concentrations in parts of the UK and which are needed for high-tech industries.'

'So we'd sell you an option on anything valuable you think might be found in the country ever again . . . in return for what?'

'Money, obviously.'

'Thank God for that.'

'A very substantial sum. Plus royalties on anything that was subsequently discovered and developed. And, at the same time, we would undertake to devote the entirety of the sum paid for the option, on behalf of the government, to protecting and enhancing the environment.'

'Is that right? And just how would that work?'

'We would take over the running of various bodies, such as the Forestry Commission, the National Parks and so on, with no management charge or fee payable by government, and with investment funds available for careful husbanding and selective development of those same assets in the best interests of both the natural environment and future generations.'

'Mr Hart – you seem to be suggesting that we give you a blank cheque on future natural resource development in the UK, in return for a large sum of money which you then spend on our behalf building country estates for your mates. Are you serious? What was your last idea?'

'My last?' I clear my throat. Even my legal team have stopped work to watch this one. 'My last . . . milord, concerns the NHS . . .'

I can feel a collective wince go round the table.

'You cunt . . .'

His gravelly northern accent cuts across me. What did he just say? Did I hear properly? I glance around the room. Everyone seems stunned. Did the minister really use the C-word? But there's more. He clears his throat and starts again, wagging his finger at me like a schoolmaster.

'You cunt be serious. This government has made its position completely clear on the NHS. One hundred per cent. So if you come in here asking me if you can approach us with some scheme to do with the NHS, you know my answer, Mr Hart.' He leans forward and looks me directly in the eye. 'You cunt.'

OK, so even I can have an off day. And if you're going to have one, go large. Do it properly. And then get arse-holed.

But on the other hand, that was extreme. And it wasn't a case of a bad northern accent. The good lord knew what he was saying. And that makes it personal.

TWO LIVERS isn't taking my calls. Who can blame her? Am I really such a useless, feckless, unreliable, shallow fool as I appear? Of course. I'm a man. I'm actually worse than I appear. Most of the time I manage to look much better than I am, because people attribute a degree of wisdom and judgment to my seniority and wealth, and so they see what they've projected onto me themselves, rather than the reality.

I leave her the inevitable grovelling messages, which I'm sure is a mistake – she doesn't do grovelling – and send flowers, the guilty man's cliché, along with perfume and a case of her favourite Chateau d'Yquem, all of which she returns without comment. I know she can't be bought, but at least I have to show I care.

After three days of being ignored, I'm desperate. So I go round to her place early in the morning and hang around on the street corner, feeling like a stalker – which, I suppose, is what I am.

I know she starts work early – most days she's at her desk around seven – and I know she works out, which is how she manages to look young and beautiful on the outside while indulging in so many vices on the inside. She punishes her body in order to remain perfect. Luckily I'm already perfect, so I don't bother. She might have a treadmill and a gym at home, but in the past she preferred to go out jogging in the mornings. If she does, I'm prepared. I have a brand new pair of Nike trainers, a tracksuit and sweat bands on both wrists. I haven't run in decades – did I ever run? – but I'm motivated, so if she appears I'll be on her tail.

And she does.

I've been hanging around since 5.30, from time to time jogging on the spot just to keep warm, ignoring other early morning runners and the odd delivery van. I'm starting to get seriously bored and thinking what a stupid idea this is, when suddenly everything happens at once.

Just after six her front door opens and a slim figure in skintight running pants, a sweatshirt, baseball cap and the obligatory earphones darts out and heads up the street, fast. I sprint after her, but she sets a killing pace and she's leaving me behind, when I benefit from divine intervention in the form of a taxi with its light on. I hail him and tell him, 'Follow that woman'. I've always wanted to do that.

We cruise down the street after her and, just as I'm thinking what a cool operator I am, she dodges down an alleyway. I pay off the cab and run after her. At the end of the alleyway she stops and lifts one leg on to the back of a bench to stretch her calf muscles.

'Hey – how are you?' I try to hide the fact that I'm gasping for breath after running barely a hundred yards.

She keeps stretching, then swaps legs. 'I stopped to give you a chance. Didn't want to kill you.'

'What do you mean?'

'You've been hanging around since 5.30. I guess you care.'

'You're damned right I care. I'm so sorry about the other night. It was a stupid fuck-up.'

'It was you, Dave. You fuck up. That's what you do.'

I feel as if she's hit me. 'So does that mean . . . ?'

'What? What does that mean?' She looks angry now. Before she was just tetchy. Now she's pissed off with me. 'Dave, you do fuck things up. All the time. But fortunately you also do other stuff as well. Great stuff. Stuff that no one else can do. That's the guy I admire. The problem is, he comes with the fuck-up as well.' She's finished stretching and goes to head off down the street. 'Don't try to keep up. I'm doing five miles and it really will kill you.'

'Oh yeah? Try me.'

I sprint off, but she passes me a few seconds later and disappears down the road and around the corner. I'm gasping already and, as soon as she's out of sight, I stop.

Phew. My legs hurt, my chest hurts and I'm sweating.

But at least we're talking again. Fuck-up? Me? Nah – just wait and see. I'm the guy who's going to get the girl.

INEFFICIENT MARKETS and bargain-hunting opportunities are natural bedfellows. The Alternative Investment Market, or AIM, is the UK's junior stockmarket, where early stage, often quite high-risk companies can list their shares in order to raise capital from investors, coincidentally generating proportionally very high fees for the brokers and advisers who work on the listing, as well as providing an opportunity for the founders of the company to raise cash by selling some of their shares. Oh, and did I mention generating very high fees for the brokers and advisers?

It's a very inefficient market, because small companies with low volumes of daily shares trading don't get the kind of investor or research analyst focus they need. After a while, they tend to be neglected to the point that their share prices drift sideways and often south, falling to levels which really don't reflect the underlying value of the business. Naturally, that doesn't matter to the advisers and brokers who persuaded them to float on AIM, because they've already banked their fees and are on to the next one.

The result is that for people with deep pockets, like me, AIM is bargain-hunting ground. A gold mine, in fact. Which is why I've decided to hoover up a bunch of gold mining stocks.

The way the mining industry works has some remarkable parallels, but also differences, compared to other industries, such as the pharmaceutical industry. Whereas big pharma depends on a constant supply of new drugs, big mining depends on a constant supply of new discoveries of proven resources – mines, to you and me – being brought into production.

But whereas big pharma does its own research and development, big mining doesn't. Instead it relies on the so-called 'juniors', small entrepreneurial mining companies that go to difficult parts of the world, exploring for new resources. Financing and refinancing themselves as they go, often on AIM, some of these companies will fail and expire, others will hit the jackpot. If they succeed, the big guys move in and buy them. It means the big guys can be fat and lazy, which they like, and only back winners, so they always look smart. The little guys, who work hard, can get very rich indeed – in their eyes, of course, not by investment banking standards – if they get lucky.

So everyone wins as long as there's a sufficient amount of luck to go round. Otherwise, the people who lose are the investors who back the juniors – the AIM investors. There are a few institutions among them, and some deal in size and understand what they're doing, but mostly we're talking members of the public who fancied a flutter and believed the bullshit some lazy journalist regurgitated from a press release issued by a financial PR firm about the next hot stock. There are so many of them out there that it really doesn't matter if a few get burnt – they're the expendable casualties of someone else's wealth-creation process.

I've summoned one of the larger AIM brokers round to my offices to listen to their best acquisition ideas in the sector. Icarus Investments not only has a reputation for fast, sharp dealings in a part of the market where you need to be quick on your feet, they also have a legendary mining-research analyst.

Mike O'Leary can drink not just for Ireland, but for the

whole of the Six Nations. He's been known to go off to international mining conferences as a keynote speaker and be so pissed he couldn't even stand, let alone talk. He once went off on a three-day bender and no one could reach him when one of their client companies was bid for. He did nothing, said nothing, spoke to no one – he couldn't, he was too pissed to talk – and while he was 'away' the bid went through after being recommended by management, and his investor clients made a fortune. When he said he couldn't remember a thing about it, they all thought he was having a laugh. By the standards of mining stockbroking, the man's a star and walks on water. His word alone, slurred as it generally is after lunch, can move markets.

When he comes to my office, just after 9.30 a.m., he's unshaven, his hair needs combing, his shirt collar is undone, his tie loosened, and he smells of alcohol. And he's the best there is, number-one-rated in his sector. Don't you just love the mining business?

His boss comes with him. Paul Summers is one of those tall, elegant, snappily dressed AIM stockbroking chief executives who could convince you that they are serious firms doing serious business. In fact if you gave him thirty seconds to prepare, he could convince anyone of anything. Flexibility is his watchword. He could sell double glazing, second-hand cars, timeshare properties on the Costa Del Sol and, in every case, after he'd closed the deal and lightened his customers' wallets, they'd be left feeling touched and grateful. He ought to be working for a major investment bank but, in the same way that pirates don't join the Royal Navy, he'd hate a large organisation.

They take a seat at the conference table and we make small talk while Maria fusses with the coffee, and they try not to stare too obviously at Happy Mboku struggling with the lunch order.

O'Leary clearly has a massive hangover, and I sympathise. He's sweating, his eyes are bloodshot, with dark rings around them, he's keeping his hands pressed firmly against the armrests of his chair, so they don't obviously shake, and I'm guessing he's as close as he wants to be to throwing up. Probably came here directly from whatever private members' club he was in last night, by the look of it, still in yesterday's clothes. We've all been there.

It's equally clear that the talking in this meeting will be done by Summers and me. O'Leary, amazingly, is here to lend credibility to the proceedings, the way top-ranked research analysts do. They're a bit like precious baubles that are nice to have and you hoard them and boast about them but don't really know quite what to do with them.

The office door opens and my legal team arrive. Four of them. These guys are drawn from DLR Strummer's mining M & A experts. Mike's probably met them before, but he doesn't recognise them in their Ray-Bans and, when they first come in, he almost panics and looks as if he might do a runner. What was he up to last night?

I do the intros and then we get straight to it.

'Paul, Mike, thank you for coming in. I want to talk gold.'

Summers goes into silky mode. 'Dave, you're certainly talking to the right people. We broke more AIM gold mining companies than the next three competitors combined. We trade more mining stocks than anyone else, we do the largest volume in the sector and, of course, Mike's reputation is second to none.'

Mike opens his mouth and looks as if he's about to say

something, but instead belches a mass of stale breath and runs for the door. Maria points him to the gents and we don't see him again, though I occasionally think I can hear someone retching massively.

Summers doesn't even pause for breath. 'Oysters.'

'Oysters?'

'He ate some bad ones last night, entertaining investor clients. Ours is a round-the-clock business, as I'm sure you understand. He didn't want to miss today's meeting, and I did warn him, but he's incredibly committed to the business. And with your reputation . . . Well, you don't need me to tell you, you're a legend. Everyone in the firm wanted to join us today when they heard about your call.'

Bring it on. I love flattery, and this guy is a second dan black belt. I can see we're going to get on well.

'Paul, roughly how many gold mining stocks are there on AIM that are under-valued relative to proven resources?'

'How many? Almost all of them. That's AIM. You know how it works. If you mean *serious* under-value, where they're starting to have targets on their backs to be taken out, I'd say, currently, about twenty.'

'And what about the Canadian exchanges? And the Aussies? How many are there in the total mining universe?'

'Again, if we're talking serious under-value, globally, perhaps fifty. A lot of people know them, of course, and are watching them. Including the mining majors. But there hasn't been much merger and acquisition activity since the credit crunch hit.'

'Excellent. I want to buy them.'

'Which ones?' His voice is a gratifying half an octave higher. The City of London is a wonderful place. It's never too late to have something completely new happen to you.

'All of them.'

'All of them?' He's almost squeaking now.

'Draw up a list. And Paul . . .'

'Dave?' He's licking his lips, nostrils slightly flared, getting excited. Really excited. He smells huge wads of cash coming his way. He's right.

'If any of these stocks starts moving before we bid, even by accident, we pull out. Of everything. I don't want any leaks to friends and family. No one gets paid back for past favours by being tipped off so they can front-run my bids.'

Paul manages to look vaguely hurt when I say this. As if he would. Yeah, right.

'We accumulate our initial positions carefully, over a few weeks, until we're ready,' I explain. 'And then, when we go, we go for all of them together, cleanly, on the same day, all over the world.'

'Multiple bids for fifty companies, all at the same time?'

'That's right. Because God is on the side of the big battalions, and weight of money always wins. No one's bigger than us. The whole sector will be re-rated after this.'

'Amen to that.'

How about that? He came in here an atheist, and now he's got religion.

I'M TRYING again with Two Livers. I've got tickets for *Figaro* at Covent Garden. I've taken a box, organised a Michelin-starred chef to provide the catering, ordered the finest wines – better than anything the Opera House ever serves – and I make sure Tom drops me off half an hour early so I can fuss unnecessarily about the details and generally irritate everyone.

On the way Tom passes me the evening paper.

'Front page news – isn't that the bloke you saw at the Treasury?'

It's true. Lord Bigmann's political career seems to have taken a bit of a dive. Apparently he's been having a little bit on the side that Lady Bigmann knew nothing about. Several little bits on the side actually, and they all look quite tasty. Someone dug up the dirt and now the papers have splashed it. In fairness, it's nothing I wouldn't do myself as a matter of daily routine, but political life in Britain is governed by a golden rule of hypocrisy: don't get caught and, if you do, make sure you're not caught doing something the Establishment – and, in particular, your political masters – might be jealous of. Lord Bigmann *did* get caught, the 'ladies' have sold their stories to the press and now there's talk of him resigning. So far Lady Bigmann is standing by her man. Looking at her picture in the paper, I wouldn't want to be in his shoes right now. She looks like she could eat a Northern scrap-metal merchant for breakfast and spit out the rusty bits. Isn't life a bitch?

Dinner at the Royal Opera House has been planned with meticulous detail. We'll start with a selection of amuse-bouches with our champagne, and then we're going to be eating foie gras terrine washed down with Tokay, followed by lobster with all kinds of interesting bells and whistles with a Grand Cru Chablis. This chef knows his stuff and I'm sure it will be a hit. As for the opera, all I have to do is not fall asleep. It's three and a half hours with one interval. I considered popping something to make sure I don't nod off, but on reflection decided to avoid drugs and alcohol altogether for twenty-four hours beforehand, and get an early night – alone – which was a challenge worth accepting for the prize I'm seeking.

So I'm feeling uncharacteristically alert and refreshed, in some ways almost disturbingly so. Without chemical assistance of one sort or another to smooth out life's little wrinkles, even small things seem to irritate me. In fact I'm pretty snappy. Chill, Hart, chill. All you have to do is stay awake and let the food, the wine and the performance take care of the rest. There's much less chance of fucking up, because most of the time you'll be sitting in silence, taking in the opera, which has great reviews and will hit the perfect cultural chord with Two Livers. The less you speak, the smaller the chance of saying the wrong thing.

The door of the box opens and I can tell she's arrived even before I turn to greet her. The trademark scent of Un Bois Vanille drifts through the box – just a hint, nothing more, because she actually knows how to wear perfume. When I turn and see her she takes my breath away. I know it sounds corny, but she truly is a vision. If I could capture the moment as she stands in the doorway, I'd carry it with me forever. She's wearing a long black satin evening dress by Stella McCartney, which opens temptingly to reveal her tanned and toned legs as she comes into the box, with a crystal pendant set with diamonds by Kiki McDonough that I bought her a couple of Christmases ago. No coincidence, and a good sign.

She steps forward and, instead of the usual air kisses, I lift her hand to my lips and kiss it. I don't think I've ever done that before to anyone, at least when I was sober.

'Thank you for coming. You look amazing.'

'Wow – peonies! Someone took some trouble.'

That would be Maria. She recalled that Two Livers loves

peonies, and rang a florist to get vases of them sent over.

'I remembered how much you like them.' OK, so I could have given Maria the credit – it would make me look generous and modest and mature and well-balanced, and all those other fine things – but I'm a banker. If I can possibly take the credit for someone else's work, I will.

'Bullshit. I bet Maria remembered. You'd never . . . well, maybe you would.' She leans forward and gives me the briefest peck on the lips. 'So are you going to pour a girl a glass of champagne?'

The great thing about a date at the opera is that it doesn't force you to deal with each other. There's the opera to talk about, to read about in the programme, to watch and listen to. Then there's the food and drink to divert you and, best of all, the people-watching. Covent Garden draws the best and worst of London society. The old Establishment have to dig deep by their standards to afford the tickets, but mandarins, academics, newspaper editors and businessmen are all there, as well as the New Money that dominates so much of London life, the arrivistes, the foreigners for whom London is a convenient bolt-hole, the tycoons and oligarchs who wouldn't know Strauss from Stravinsky. And, of course, the City is there too. In the City, cultural pretensions are an essential item to acquire once you've done money – part of the means by which you show you've arrived, you're not just a one-dimensional banker but a rounded, cultured, elevated individual who understands and appreciates the finer things of life. Even if you haven't a clue what's going on and find it hell to have to turn your Blackberry off for three and a half hours.

So I'm surprised when, towards the end of the interval, as we're sipping fine wine and talking about the performance

– and no, I haven't fallen asleep – Two Livers seems distracted, partly absent from the conversation.

'What's up? Am I boring you?'

'Not yet.'

Ouch. I look hurt, and she laughs.

'Joke. Relax. I'm not bored with you. Ever. So long as you don't try to be someone else, that is. You're Dave Hart. You're exceptional and you're interesting, and you've done amazing things. And deep down you're capable of being quite decent. By City standards, anyway.'

What's going on? I'm not sure how to respond. I think those were all compliments. And what does she mean by 'deep down'? I don't have a deep down.

'Is that what you're afraid of – boredom?'

'Isn't everyone?' She looks me squarely in the eye. 'Aren't you?'

'Yes. All the time. Every day of my life. But how do you deal with it? How to keep the demons at bay? They're always there, you know. Only a heartbeat away.'

She takes my hand and we have beautiful eye contact. I wish more women did that. I can feel a stirring. This could be a great night.

'Dave, you keep the demons away for me. I never know what the hell you'll do next. Probably most of the time you don't know yourself. But there's always something. Always.'

She's right. I hadn't thought about it before. Probably because deep down I'm too shallow. 'I know. I can't sit still. Ever. Otherwise, what's life for?'

She's squeezing my hand now and nods towards the stage. 'Do you really want to see the second half?'

'Not if the alternative is going back to your place.'

'Let's go.'

Fuck the opera. Mind you, it did the trick.

'THIS ACTION in the mining sector is amazing. You sure know how to make an impact.'

I'm having breakfast at George on Mount Street with Arthur Morgan, an American ex-hedge fund manager.

Arthur is still only thirty-six years old, but he has grey hair and worry lines. He's had a tough couple of years. He's effectively been through the entire cycle of the hedge fund industry. He started as a trader at Schleppenheim, got promoted early on because he was good, and then left to start his own fund. In those early days, he was what used to be called a new-issue 'flipper'. The market was hot for new issues of shares, especially by high-tech companies, and some of these shares would see their prices soar by fifty per cent or more on the first day of trading. Some even doubled. People who bought them at the issue price could sell them – flip them – the same day for a huge profit. The big investment banks allocated these shares to their favourite clients, and people like Arthur made sure they were the favourite clients. If they got an allocation, they guaranteed to give the firm in question a big chunk of their profit back in brokerage commission on other business in the market. This kept the firms happy, ensured that the flipper kept getting allocations, and everyone made out like bandits. The only people paying for the party were the companies whose shares were underpriced when they came to market, but since this is something most companies only do once, and a soaring share price is seen as success, they didn't mind being raped. In fact, they rather liked it.

And, of course, the new-issue flippers made sure they

gave the best parties and invited all the key decision makers from the big banks. They even let some of those people invest in their funds, allegedly at times on preferential terms.

It was all too good to last, and eventually, about a decade into this great new game, word filtered through to the regulators and they finally party-pooped the whole thing. Allocations of hot new stocks could no longer be tied to brokerage commissions and other perceived inducements were cracked down on. The idea that key personnel in the investment banks could profit alongside the funds they were allocating hot stocks to was banned (it had actually always been banned, but there are bans and there are bans).

So the smart money moved on. Arthur got into managed futures, running highly technical, trend-following macro strategies that allowed him to benefit from whatever was happening in the markets by doing the same thing as quickly as possible after it had already happened in the markets, and hoping to profit sufficiently by the time the trend changed, so that he could bank a decent return.

Great idea, until the crunch came and suddenly trends went haywire, losses piled up and Arthur found himself dealing with a bunch of people who'd invested in his fund and now wanted their money back. Being an honourable man, he gave it back. Others 'closed' their funds to redemptions, but he didn't and lost most of the money he was running and found the business could no longer cover its overheads – or his lifestyle. He personally paid off all the creditors and wound it up, honour intact but wallet empty.

So now he's a specialist headhunter for the hedge fund industry. He's quite successful because he's got the credibility of someone who's worn the T-shirt himself, and somehow he manages not to puke when he has to pander to some of the strutting teenage egos who appoint him to hire smart people on their behalf.

'SO FAR so good,' I tell him. 'The mining thing's worked out well. On paper we're well up, but bid timetables are frustrating and nothing's over 'til it's over.'

'Dave, the compliment's a genuine one. You came back from . . .' He's at a bit of a loss as to what to say next.

'The dead.'

He laughs, and it does seem genuine. 'You came back from the dead, raised the biggest fund anyone can remember, and now you're swinging that money around like crazy. It's amazing. Your fund is moving markets and changing the way things are done. First conglomerates, now mining.'

I could sit here and absorb compliments all day. Especially real ones from someone who doesn't think he's going to get anything out of me except breakfast. Unfortunately, I'm quite distracted by the newspaper. It's the latest in the Bigmann saga. The *Daily Post* is carrying an exclusive about how the good lord was salting away money on the side in the Turks and Caicos Islands for years before entering politics. Tax dodging the old-fashioned way, not even very smart, and it probably wouldn't make the front page if he didn't have a 'tax adviser' who looks stunning in a tiny bikini.

Normally these things are kept discreet, but someone must have found her and persuaded her to spill the beans – and do a great photo shoot on the beach in the Caribbean with a photographer, a make-up artist, wardrobe, design, lighting . . . Poor Lord Bigmann. An unlikely Lothario, with his huffing and puffing – must be Viagra. Probably feeling like a marked man now.

The tax adviser in the bikini managed to push the day's other big story off the front page. On page two there's an article about some rap artists who've been caught with one of the biggest hauls of cocaine ever discovered in the UK: more than half a ton, with a street value of over thirty million pounds. The plods think they were using their nationwide tour to distribute it on an industrial scale. They're denying it – well, they would, wouldn't they? – and claiming a stitch-up, but the coke is real, it's huge, and whoever has that kind of money to throw around just to stitch someone up? I hope the D Boyz look good in orange pyjama suits with HMP on the back.

But I don't have all day to muse. I turn to Arthur. 'That's what I wanted to talk about. The fund management industry. Where does it go next?'

'I'm not sure it has to go anywhere. It went through a rough patch in the credit crunch, but that was to be expected. Fortunately, people have short memories. They're still paying crazy fees to a bunch of kids for taking their money and going to the casino with it. Life is good, at least in hedge fund world.'

'So where does the innovation come from? How does the industry continue to justify those fees?'

'It doesn't. You don't change a perfect scam unless you have to. There are always smart new people entering the industry, of course, but they generally get picked up early on by the big players and put to work as slave labour with minimal share of the economics. But they're wannabes, so they can hardly complain.'

'That's exactly what I was thinking, Arthur. The people

who run these firms think they're God. Some may indeed be quite good, but most are mediocre, and a few are really crap, but they take big gambles which, in good times, with strong markets, tend to work out. They cream it off, knowing they're only a second away from the world waking up and saying to them, "Guys, you're stark naked." So they don't really build their firms, don't invest for the future in growing their own young talent within the firm. And that's the opportunity.'

'What opportunity?'

'The opportunity to mount a raid, to poach the number twos who actually do most of the work and the smart newcomers who'll never be given their head.'

'But which firm are you talking about, Dave? Do you have someone in mind?'

'All of them.'

'All of them? But there are hundreds. Do you want to go after them all?'

'Why not?'

'What would you do with them?'

'I'd put them in a huge warehouse full of computer screens and phones – let's call it a trading floor. I'd give them capital to trade however they want and a really bright boss who'd keep an eye on them, making sure none of them went nuts and getting them to stay within their trading limits. The ones who did well, I'd give them half of what they made. I'd take any losses on their behalf.'

'Sounds like a good deal.' Arthur rubs his chin. I like it when people rub their chins in meetings with me. 'And who would run it?'

'You know who'd run it. You'd do it for a percentage. You'd have to give up headhunting – once you'd completed this last assignment, that is.'

'But these hedgies, the bosses whose talent we'd be poaching, they'd sue.' Nice touch that – now it's 'we'. 'They're brats. If they don't get their own way, they're the first to stamp their feet and run home crying for mummy. And they always reach for their lawyers.'

'I have lawyers too. An army of them. The biggest law firm in the world. Literally thousands upon thousands. And I love a fight.'

'OK, so where do we take this?'

'Before we do that, there's one thing you have to understand, Arthur.'

'What's that?'

'No shorting. We're only going to invest in the long side of the market. We're going to run strategies that involve buying things that we expect to go up, rather than selling things to make them go down. The Salvation Fund invests for good. I know it sounds corny, but I don't want us to profit out of someone else's misfortune. When a company's share price falls, no one on my team will be cheering. I'm even planning a campaign to get short-selling banned in the London market.'

'Are you serious?'

'Sure, I'm serious. My PR guys are briefing MPs already. We'll hold off from getting this into the press until we're ready. Then we hit the hedgies with an industry-wide talent raid, as well as a political campaign to get half their business abolished or forced offshore.'

'You'd really force them out?'

'*I* wouldn't. Politicians would. By accident. Look what they did to the non-doms. Politicians never really know what they're doing until after it's happened. But that doesn't matter, because London would be a better place. Imagine what would happen if thousands of hedgies moved offshore. Normal people would be able to get tables at decent restaurants again – and Wimbledon tickets, and Glyndebourne. Think what it would do to Chelsea house prices. Real people would be able to afford to live in Chelsea again.'

'Dave . . . would that be a good thing?'

'Not sure. Let me think about that one.'

I'M SEEING Two Livers again tonight. We're having dinner, but not at some fancy restaurant. She's cooking for me. This is a very good sign. I don't know how great a cook she is, but since she does everything else superbly, I'm guessing that it will be pretty tasty. And since we'll already be at her place, it won't be far from the dining room to the bedroom.

Tom picks me up at seven and has a twinkle in his eye as he asks me what sort of dinner party it is – business or pleasure?

'Put it this way – it's just the two of us.' At least I hope it is. What if I get there and it's one of those horrible surprise parties, where all kinds of people you don't want to see have been invited and, because they felt they couldn't tell whoever was organising it that they didn't want to see you either, they've actually made an effort and come?

Nah, impossible. It'll just be the two of us. I'm sure of it. Why would she want to invite anyone else when she's got me?

I decide I need some assertive displacement activity to fill the momentary void and overcome my uncertainty, so I text her: 'ON MY WAY. X.' Why do I do that? And why the capitals? Is it really to be assertive? To reassure myself? Or so she has plenty of time to get her lover out the back door? Or to get all the 'surprise guests' into the back room with the light turned off?

No. It's just the two of us.

Tom drops me off, I ring the bell and wait impatiently for what I'm sure is just a few seconds, but seems longer.

I'm gazing back down the street when the door opens and, without looking, I say, 'Darling, these are for you,' and hand a large bunch of peonies and a bottle of Krug to . . . a waiter. A uniformed waiter. For just the two of us? Damn. 'What are you doing here?'

He looks uncomfortable, takes the flowers and champagne, and shows me inside. No thank you, pal. I already know the way inside. I've been here before. I've even made love to your employer.

When I enter the drawing room, there are two other couples there. What the fuck is going on? A young guy in a Richard James suit with a pale purple shirt, undone enough to show a bunch of chest hair that I really didn't need him to share with me, seems to be paired up with a leggy brunette about three inches taller than him, in flat shoes and a long black sequinned number which I don't recognise and can't be bothered staring at. Next to them is an older man with his back to me when I come in. He turns and, thank God, it's the Silver Fox – with his latest squeeze, who I believe is a twenty-three-year-old Spanish girl. She certainly has the flashing dark eyes and mane of long black hair, and she oozes passion and temperament.

'Dave, come in. Laura's in the kitchen working her magic. Let me introduce you to people.' His squeeze I take in, because who couldn't, and I mumble something to the other woman, Sarah, but I'm mostly trying not to show my disappointment. Then we turn to chest hair. 'Dave, can I introduce you to Sir Neil Moreland? Have you met before?'

Sir Neil Moreland? *Sir* fucking Neil Moreland? This kid's younger than me. What's he doing with a fucking knighthood? Inwardly I scratch my head. I've heard of Neil Moreland. He used to be some kind of athlete – won a gold medal in the Olympics for . . . something or other. Then he went into business, started his own firm – I think it was sports related, a chain of gyms, or maybe it was retail – and sold out for a fortune so he could sail round the world. When he came back, he bought back his old business for a song, it having fallen on hard times without his hand on the tiller, and now he's motoring again. And he's got a knighthood for services to . . . sport? Maybe. Business? Possibly. Party donations? Almost definitely. Why is he here? Why couldn't Two Livers and I have had a quiet dinner *à deux* and then gone to bed?

'Pleased to meet you, Sir Neil. I'm Dave. Dave Hart.'

'Delighted to meet you, Dave. I've heard a lot about you. And, please, just Neil is fine.'

Very fucking condescending of you, sir. Thank you very fucking much, sir. Let me tug my fucking forelock, sir. Why am I here? I feel like going home.

But then the door opens and I know why I'm here.

She's wearing a black floral lace negligee dress with the same jewellery by Kiki that she wore to the opera. The dress is sufficiently see-through to be exciting and she's bra-less underneath. A woman needs a lot of confidence to wear a dress like that. Models can get away with it on the catwalk, but in real life most women wouldn't dare and most men can only dream. But she isn't most women. Irritatingly, I can't place the designer. I'm not on form tonight. She smiles and greets, sharing a few private words with each of the guests, while I hold back, waiting 'til last.

'How are you, Dave?' She kisses me on each cheek. Her scent tantalises me, and I'm tempted to grab her and kiss her firmly on the lips, ignoring the others. But I don't. I've no idea what it is she's planning tonight, but I don't think that's on the menu.

'I'm great. I wasn't expecting –'

'Has everyone got a drink?' Before I can finish she's off, looking after everyone – everyone except me – changing the music, asking what the bimbos like listening to – as if anyone cared – pouring more drinks and joking with the Silver Fox. Who is his biggest client, for fuck's sake? I bet I've paid him more fees than his next ten clients combined. At least I hope I have. I like to be able to count on people's attention.

They're all talking about the Bigmann resignation. There have even been calls for him to be stripped of his peerage, which is apparently quite hard to do. The final straw was when the press found he had a couple of love children in Spain and photographed them with their mothers – photogenic Northern lasses who were happy to relocate, with a wedge in the bank and a big monthly cheque, to villas that were conveniently (for him) close to each other. Why would they come forward now? I guess someone with an even bigger wallet must have found them and offered them an even bigger wedge. Success is so fickle. Here one day, gone the next. It's a funny old world.

Sir Neil sidles up to me. 'So, Dave, not many people get to come back from the dead.'

Jesus Christ. Good opening, pal. Like I haven't heard that anywhere before.

'Really? Is that what you believe?'

He pauses and looks at me. 'What do you believe?'

'I'm not sure. I believe we're all on a journey. Where it takes us, how far and what happens, is impossible to predict. But I don't see death as a final barrier. I think there might be a higher purpose.' I turn to his companion, who has wandered over to join us. 'What do you think, milady?'

'It's Sarah, please.'

He looks uneasy and feels he has to say something. 'Sarah and I aren't married.' So he hasn't married her? Now there's a surprise. Maybe he's not so dumb, after all. Women like her are like fruit machines. Put anything you like in the slot. Just not your money. But then he goes and blows it. 'But we've been together a long time.' Probably seems like a long time.

'So he hasn't made a lady out of you? I bet a lot of men would love the chance.' She flashes a glance at him. Bingo. 'So what's your view on . . . life, Sarah? Or maybe death? Is this it? Is this what it's all about?'

She's clearly been hanging around too long with a rich, successful, well-connected man, because she mistakes me taking the piss for a genuine enquiry, as if I might really have the slightest interest in her views on anything at all, or even give her the time of day if she wasn't with him, and therefore, here tonight. Cute she might be, but the reality is she's an Insignificant Other. Cruel? Me? Just honest. Welcome to London Society.

'I . . . uh . . .' She looks at *Sir* Neil. 'I agree with you. I think we're all on a journey too.'

Smart girl.

I'm about to fire the next salvo and can tell *Sir* Neil thinks it unfair that I'm using her rather than going at him mano-a-mano, but who cares?

Obviously Two Livers cares. Her antennae have been twitching, probably spotted something about the body language, contempt and loathing and all that, and she comes over to intervene. What is it with people at dinner parties? Dinner parties are just another form of competition, another way for guys to wave their willies – mine is bigger than yours, my life is amazing, yeah, yeah. We were bored by this bullshit when we first heard it a thousand years ago. And who on earth brought us together thinking that, for some bizarre reason, we'd get on and have any interest whatsoever in each other? We're men. We're juvenile, immature, full of testosterone. We want to arm wrestle or roll around on the ground trying to strangle each other.

Well, on second thoughts, Two Livers brought us together. And she's not dumb. I look again at him.

'Neil, what are you up to these days? I guess you still work out. You look like you're in pretty good shape.' A little flattery never hurt anyone. *Sir* Neil laps it up.

'I still train hard.' He pats his ironing-board stomach. 'Try to stay fit, though it gets harder every year.'

I rub my martini gut. 'Yeah, me too. Doesn't get any easier.'

I think I'm trying hard to establish common ground between us, but he thinks I've relapsed into taking-the-piss mode.

'Are you a sportsman, Dave?'

'Used to be. Not any more. Now I get all my exercise lying down.'

Before I can ask him about his sex life and dust off all

those old horizontal jogging jokes, Two Livers intervenes again.

'I think it's time we sat down. Would everyone like to come through?'

Dinner is amazing. We start with white asparagus with foie gras, followed by chilled carrot soup, and then roast pigeon as the main course. And it's all superb. How does she do it? I couldn't. I probably didn't need to tell you that. What's interesting is that every dish has some individual, special feature, something surprising and deliciously tempting. Or maybe it's just that it's perfectly prepared. She must have been working for hours and planned this for days. But it's worth it. When you dine out constantly in over-priced, pretentious restaurants, your appetite becomes jaded. You become completely saturated, so that it's hard to enjoy anything at all without finding some imaginary fault. So when I'm completely blown away by a meal, it's a rare event. Two Livers has excelled. She has the waiter to help serve and clear away the dishes, but otherwise just goes to and from the kitchen in an unhurried, completely confident way. This is a dinner party. She's the hostess. Where's the stress? Where's the pressure? Something must have gone wrong. Something always does. But not tonight.

So I find myself not only noticing the food, but positively enjoying it. The wine is perfectly chosen, but I expected that and help myself liberally. The Silver Fox keeps us all entertained with his never-ending fund of stories and, to my surprise, I'm having a good time. At a dinner party. This might be the first time ever.

And then, at Two Livers' prompting, *Sir* Neil starts talking about sport. She glances my way to see how pissed I am and whether I'm actually listening, and I frown to look like I'm concentrating and lean my head to one side to show sympathy and empathy and understanding. As if. I'm here, Neil, and I'm paying attention.

'. . . So the sports industry – if you can call it that – never really integrated. You have manufacturers and retailers, the way you do in other industries, and then you have the clubs and the stars – the talent, if you like. Some of these are big businesses, like Premier League football clubs, but they're generally rich men's indulgences rather than viable businesses, run mostly for the benefit of the players' and their agents' wallets. But a lot of talent doesn't get support. Look at amateur athletics. Track and field events are hugely neglected. And swimming. Huge numbers of people participate, especially young people, but there's a disconnect between them and the world of business. And the reason is the media, which is a massive business in its own right. They can make or break a sport with their coverage, but their programming is dominated by a handful of high-profile events – football, tennis, Formula One, probably half a dozen others.'

'Figure skating.' It's Sarah, his squeeze. The one he won't marry.

'What?' He looks irritated.

'I said figure skating.' I think she's pissed.

'No. Figure skating doesn't get the coverage. It could probably do with it, but it doesn't get it. It proves my point.'

'Oh.' She looks crestfallen. Keep hitting the juice, babe. We're on to dessert and we'll all be going home soon.

'We have very expensive in-depth coverage of a few sports, but we're missing the breadth.'

Interesting. He sounds like he cares.

'I have a question,' I pipe up. He looks at me as if I'm going to make another of my arsehole remarks. Understandable. 'Don't people get the sports coverage they deserve? If there's enough interest, won't the media follow the market? And won't manufacturers and retailers do the same?'

He takes a moment before answering, obviously wondering what my angle is. I must be taking the piss, but it seems like a genuine question.

'The media don't follow the public. It's the other way round. The media have got so big that they create the market. They create the super-brands in sport, whether it's clubs or individuals, and the manufacturers and retailers follow them. The public get the sport they're given, not the sport they deserve or would necessarily choose if they were asked.'

'So fix the media and you fix the problem?'

He's still suspicious. What's the punchline? Where's the put-down coming from?

'Dave, no one can fix the media.' Now he sounds condescending. Careful, pal. 'It's the ultimate big business. They're huge, highly concentrated – probably more than is good for us in a theoretically free and democratic society, and they have big cheque books.'

'Mine's bigger.'

'What do you mean?'

'My cheque book. I've got the biggest one.'

He rolls his eyes. So this is it? This was my point? Just when he thought I was being serious.

'No, he means it.' It's Two Livers, and she reaches out and touches Neil briefly on the arm to reassure him. 'His really is huge.'

Now he's glancing at her, wondering if we're in this together. I need to show him I'm real.

'Neil, think of all the money you can possibly imagine. Mountains of it. Then double it. Well, I have more.' Me and the cartels and the syndicates and the crime families and all of their buddies. We're in this together.

He pushes his chair back from the table and wipes his face with his napkin. I can see he doesn't get it.

'Neil, I have a fund. A very large fund. We can invest in anything we want. We raised eighteen billion dollars for our first closing a few months ago, and so far we're well up performance-wise. Our investors are very happy and I could easily go to them for another eighteen billion. Or more. In fact, in a few weeks I probably will. I just need a sufficiently compelling proposition and I'll do it.'

It's true. The normal 'friction cost' of moving illegal money into the legitimate economy – drug profits, say, or money acquired through racketeering – is thirty to forty per cent. But once these guys have established a genuine route to change black money into clean, legally earned profits accrued within my fund – which is, in any case, showing a great return – they won't want to stop. Why would they? They'd happily put everything through me.

'Do you mean it?'

'Neil, I never joke about money.'

THERE WAS a postscript.

When the other guests had left, and Two Livers and I were alone, and I was thanking her, because I really do want to do something with Neil and his ideas on sports and media, I poured myself a Scotch from her drinks cabinet and went to the kitchen looking for ice – where I found a bunch of guys in chefs' outfits packing up cooking utensils.

'Who are you?'

One of them held his hand out. I'm sure I've seen him before. Some kind of TV chef. 'We were cooking for you this evening.'

What can I say? I laugh. No wonder she looked calm and unflustered. 'Guys, it was amazing. Great food. Blew me away. Do you do this all the time?'

'Only for special clients.'

When I go back to the drawing room, she's changed into a silk robe and she's curled up on the sofa.

'I know your secret.'

'Are you sure?' She almost purrs the words. I sit beside her and she reaches out to stroke my leg and runs her fingernails up the inside of my thigh. I love it when a woman makes the first move. Especially a move like that. 'Which one?'

'The chefs. Just met them in the kitchen. They did a great job.'

She laughs. 'Oh, that secret. I don't mind you knowing *that* secret.'

'Do you have any others?'

She leans across and, just as our lips meet, she whispers, 'Thousands. More than you can ever imagine.'

IF YOU know everything about a woman, your relationship with her is already over. On to the next. Or maybe not. Maybe you've married her and got kids and the two of you stay together, but the magic is over and the fire's gone out. But until you reach that stage, there's always something elusive, something to go for that you haven't yet grasped.

So I'm sat at my desk twiddling my thumbs, tormenting myself by wondering what secrets Two Livers has that I don't know about. Men, certainly. She's known a few, more than a few actually, and I don't mind that. She's a woman of the world, a modern-day female predator in a way that used to be reserved exclusively for guys. I like that.

Hmm. Secrets. Women? For sure. At least once with me in a threesome, and it can't have been the first time. Does that bother me? Quite the opposite. It's exciting. I wish more women did it.

Drugs? I'm hardly in a position to complain. And she uses far less than I do.

Booze? Of course. But she seems to have an iron constitution. And she works out. She's in seriously good shape.

So what other secrets could there be? She's not a gambler, not in a regular sense. She'll enjoy a night out at the casino, and she'll take risks at work which would make a lot of people's hair stand on end. But nothing I have a problem with. Again, I admire what she does.

Significant others lurking in the background? None that I know of, and I had her checked out years ago by an agency.

Maybe she wants to start a family. She may feel the biological clock is ticking, she isn't getting any younger – all that shit professional women on the career ladder torture themselves with. Only she's already rich and successful, certainly enough to make whatever choices she wants, including starting a family if she wants to. And, anyway, she's still in her thirties and has years yet.

Would I want to start a family with her? I already have a daughter I barely know. I feel . . . indifferent. But I

124

could have children again. Why not? I assume we'd delegate childcare to hired help the way successful people do these days, limiting our involvement to parents' evenings and nativity plays and stage-managed competitive birthday parties with other parents and, of course, plenty of photo shoots to show how happy and united we are and how much we love each other. So I guess that isn't a problem.

But what about her fears? Has she been let down by a man? Must have been. We've been doing it for millions of years and I don't see why she should be immune. But, on the other hand, she's resilient. She'd bounce back, devour or discard the man who had failed her, and move on.

Boredom, or fear of it, seems to be the demon she most has to slay. That's a common bond between us, not something that's likely to be a problem. We even started to talk about it at the opera, and I'm happy sharing it with her. I could never be alone with myself. I always need company, diversions, new sources of stimulation. Stand still and you die, or you might as well.

So I'm left cluelessly staring at a blank screen, when Sir Neil Moreland and his team arrive. They sit down in the conference room. Maria makes sure they are happy and then taps on my door to remind me that it's me they've come to see.

This time I'm determined to get on well with Neil. I want us to be on the same team, pointing in the same direction and facing down the same enemies. So I'm polite and smile a lot at the kids he's brought with him – his commercial director and his creative director, whatever the hell those titles mean. His people are clearly fascinated by my team in the dealing room.

'Who are those people? What are they doing?'

Happy and the guys are on a conference call, shouting and stomping around. From time to time Happy raises a giant fist and smashes it down on the desk. It's quite impressive, but gets better when somebody passes Nob a short plank of wood and he puts it between two desks and screams then breaks it in two with his head.

'Ordering lunch. They're my traders. They mostly just order lunch. It gets delivered. The big black guy – he's Happy. You'll be working a lot with him if we do this.'

'Happy?'

'That's his name. Happy Mboku. You can see he's happy. You just don't want to catch him on a bad day. And the tall Japanese guy – he's Nob. You'll be working with him too.'

'Nob? Do we call him Nob?'

'You can if you want.'

Someone's passed Nob an empty beer bottle. He picks it up by the neck, shouts something warlike in Japanese and smashes it over his head.

'Christ.' Neil seems a bit put off by Nob, who's waving around the shattered remains of the bottle like an improvised weapon. 'Are you sure they're safe?'

'Totally. At least when they know they have food coming. Although I tend not to go in there myself. Not until they've eaten, anyway.'

'Does he often do that with beer bottles?'

'Sure. And wine, champagne . . . pretty much anything. Apparently it's all down to technique. Anyone can do it.'

Neil's team shake their heads and I guess that they won't be asking Nob to teach them.

We go through a longer and much less exciting version of what Neil laid out over dinner. The kids are so serious and well intentioned about the whole thing that I start to get bored. They've brought a Powerpoint and it looks like ninety slides. After an hour, we're only on slide forty. This really won't do. We're only talking a few billion and I don't have all day. I have to take charge before I lose the will to live.

'Thanks, guys, that was fantastic.'

They look up at me, guppy-like, and then at their boss. They haven't finished yet, not even halfway through. I know. That's the point.

'Neil, let's cut to the chase. We need to go after a few media companies. TV, radio, print media. Because there are ownership and control restrictions, we mustn't bid to take them over, just acquire significant minority stakes and then have the kind of conversations that get people's attention. Make them compliant, shall we say? In parallel, we go for one of the big sports apparel companies, take it over and fold in your retail chain. A lot of investment follows to make both state of the art. We invest in advertising and promoting the brands, and go online in a big way. Then we roll out one new minority sport a month on TV, with high-profile sponsorship, celebs, fanfare, razzmatazz, blah, until we run out of sports. Which will be never. We position ourselves to be best placed in the market to satisfy the demand generated by greater participation – we sell people the shirts, the shorts, the trainers, or whatever it is they need. And we set up a foundation that makes sure we tick the political boxes with scholarships for talented kids, prizes, social inclusion and all that useful bullshit. Back of an envelope, we're talking five billion?'

He nods. He looks quite excited.

'OK, let's do it.'

The great thing about being unaccountable is that you can do any damned thing you like.

I'M AT Duke's, sitting at a corner table, while Alessandro pours weapons-grade martinis for Arthur Morgan and me. Arthur's had the craziest few weeks of his career. After our meeting, he drew up a list of more than a hundred key people in number two or three positions at hedge funds, plus another list of more junior people who looked to be smart and hungry. Then he hired a couple more headhunting firms, this being a labour-intensive business, and started sounding people out, having discreet conversations, drawing up draft offer letters and agreeing numbers.

Then on Monday, a week ago, he hit them all with firm 'exploding' offers. Join today and it's a deal. Hesitate and it's *sayonara*. He got seventy per cent acceptances, and a new trading floor I've taken just off St James's Square is filling up nicely.

Word spreads quickly in the hedge fund community. Email, text, Bloomberg and plain old-fashioned phone calls act like jungle drums. 'Joe is leaving Vampire.' 'Mick quit Hercules.' And so on. After a while, even hedgies worked out that it was a pretty unusual day. Everyone seemed to be moving. Or maybe just leaving. And it wasn't the 'names' that were going. Who'd want them? It was the real people. The ones who did the work and achieved the performance. Dozens of them.

Was it because of all this political stuff in the papers? Surely no one would actually ban short selling? Even politicians couldn't be that dumb, could they?

And slowly word spread. It was Dave Hart, and he was

turning his attention to the hedge fund industry. A dozen lawsuits followed. Predatory hiring practices, incitement to breach contracts, blah, blah. That's why I have DLR Strummer. For every suit they have a team, and every team is ready to go to war with claims and counter-claims, defending the right of free people to choose their place of employment. Meanwhile, waiting in the wings is the Silver Fox, ready to spread the word, if they cut up rough, that drive-by capital has lost its key people and may no longer be viable – as if he would.

I like causing consternation. I like shaking things up. Now when I walk down St James's Street on my way to Duke's, I get angry looks from guys in pin-striped suits with white shirts and open necks. People I've never even met don't like me. Successful, rich, talented people who never had it so good suddenly need to work again. Hands on. Because all the smart young guys have left and the price of talent just went up.

Arthur and I raise our glasses and he proposes a toast.

'Health, wealth and happiness.'

I shake my head. 'No. Wealth, health, even more wealth, and then happiness can take care of itself.'

The first sip of a martini is always the best, just as the first kiss is the most enticing. We pause for a moment in silent respect and then get down to business.

'Arthur, how long 'til you start trading?'

'Less than a month. An amazing number of the guys are only on a month's notice with no non-compete language in their contracts. Their bosses didn't want to have to pay them to keep them offside, so they're free. We have the systems set up and we'll tuck in under your regulatory authorisation.'

'Excellent. I love it when a plan comes together.' I take a second sip.

'Are you going to come over to the offices to see things?'

'No. Not unless I need to. If you have a good man in charge, give him his head.' It sounds as if I'm a great delegator, doesn't it? But really I'm just lazy.

'So, Dave, what are you going to do? What's next?'

'I've always been a bit of a sportsman, as you know.' Arthur tries not to choke on his martini. 'I'm looking at sports and media. I think there are some big opportunities there. But it's a new world for me. I need to meet the people, check it out, do my homework, you know.'

'I'm sure you'll have a great time. Although . . . media people are different.'

'Oh, come on, Arthur. They can't be that different. We're all built the same way. We all have the same DNA. And I find I can get along with most people if I try hard enough.'

He looks concerned. 'Don't be so sure, Dave. You might have to try really, really hard. These guys live in a world apart. Bankers and hedgies might be bad, but media people are bad and dumb at the same time.'

Really? Now I'm intrigued. This could be more interesting than I thought. Better have another martini.

I'VE COME to visit Charles Merton. Charles runs sports coverage at MileHigh TV, one of the biggest satellite broadcasters. MileHigh have the kind of offices in West London that give glitz a bad name – shiny marble and chrome and plate glass on a scale that is meant to be futuristic, but instead strikes me as soulless and insubstantial. There are no reference points in a building like this, no heart. You could change the name at the front and install a sanitaryware manufacturer and no one would be any the wiser. I guess that's showbiz.

Neil Moreland is with me and he seems nervous. Why? I think the reason is that Merton is both hugely powerful in broadcasting – his decisions on what to cover and when can sink or swim a major sporting event – and has a notoriously massive ego. I tell Neil to relax – we have massive egos too. Everything will be fine.

I'm wrong. There, I said it. I'm not often wrong – I think the last time was back in the nineties – but this time I definitely am.

Merton keeps us waiting in his outer office for half an hour. I don't mind too much, because he has a stunning eye-candy sex-bomb secretary, who keeps crossing and uncrossing her very long legs in her very short skirt and casting glances in my direction. When we first arrived, she asked if I was *the* Dave Hart. Normally, if someone asks that I say no, I'm the other one, but instead I gave her a winning smile and nodded. Neil didn't like that, because he's very competitive and probably a little immature when it comes to these things, but I made a note to send her a whole van full of flowers and a thank-you note when I got back to the office. I'm not immature at all when it comes to women.

So we sit and watch a giant-screen TV showing non-stop MileHigh News. They have breaking news from Pentonville Prison, where some famous rap star who got banged up on drugs charges tried to hang himself. Apparently he'd been made to share a cell with a lifer from the Russian Mafia who was given a very rare whole life tariff by the judge who sentenced him, because he not only cut his rivals' heads off but cooked and ate them as well. Once upon a time he was in the illegal diamond trade, but now he spends all day working out in the prison gym and apparently never sleeps. They show his face and he does look very pale, a bit like one of Rom's undead. I suppose those guys don't sleep, and you wouldn't want to share a cell with one of them for very long, would you? I mean, anything could happen. And probably did, any number of times. But why would any prison officer with half a brain put the rapper in with a guy like this? Probably because prison officers make less than thirty grand a year with overtime and they want to enjoy the good things in life, the same as the rest of us.

We can tell Merton is in his office, because other people go in and out from time to time, some of them glancing dismissively in our direction, most ignoring us, and we can hear him talking on the phone, laughing and chatting about his weekend plans and other shit. Apparently he's going to Dubai and he's booked a penthouse suite at the Al Khalid Hotel, the tallest hotel in the city, looking out over the Gulf. I hope he has a head for heights.

When he finally summons us, he doesn't get up from his seat or offer to shake hands, just points to a couple of very low chairs in front of his desk and says, 'Sit.'

Do I look like a fucking dog? Is he trying to piss us off? Even I don't behave this badly. Welcome to the world of media. Merton is a kid in his thirties with slicked back hair, apparently a wunderkind of the TV world, and he's dressed completely in black. Ugh. Didn't anyone tell him new media black went out when people stopped talking about new media?

'So what do you want?'

That's it? That's the fucking pleasantries? No 'Hi, I'm Charles. Sorry I kept you guys waiting, but I'm an arsehole and I do that kind of shit to people I don't know because I figure that if they don't already exist within my tiny universe they can't be very important'? Not even a cup of coffee? Oh, but there is coffee. He has a cup already, and as we sit down he pours himself a refill from a flask on his desk, but doesn't offer us any. Wanker.

Neil doesn't blink, just goes into a whole spiel about how the Salvation Fund is looking to invest in MileHigh stock, how we're aiming to expand sports coverage into minority sports and planning on backing up our interest with a charitable foundation that will support social inclusion and various other important-sounding objectives wrapped up in third-sector speak.

Because he's nervous, and this obviously matters to him an awful lot, he gets tongue-tied. While the passion is still there, his nervousness shows through and he becomes uncharacteristically inarticulate. In the end he does a poor job – five out of ten? – which pisses me off even more, not because I care how well he does, but because he shouldn't be intimidated by a wanker like this.

It doesn't matter. Merton doesn't even pretend to listen. He plays on his fucking Blackberry the whole way through. It even buzzes at him and he grins as he replies to whichever fucking real person he's communicating with – as opposed to the two dummies he's sitting with now.

'OK, guys, that's it.'

What? What just happened?

'Time's up. Thank you very much for coming. Carole will show you out.'

I don't get this. Neil has laid out the plan, Merton's failed to listen or comment and now he's showing us out? Is that it?

I clear my throat. 'Mr Merton . . . thank you for your time. We really appreciated it. I couldn't help overhearing just now that you're planning to be in Dubai this weekend. Staying at the Al Khalid. I've heard great things about it.'

He plainly hates having to delay clearing his office to make small talk with a non-person. 'That's right,' he grunts.

'It's very tall.'

'Yes, it is.' Now he thinks he's dealing with a real fucking dummy. 'The tallest hotel in the whole of the Gulf. I've booked the penthouse.' He can't resist adding that fine little detail. Nice. Thank you, pal.

'Look out for one of my colleagues while you're there. A big black guy. Happy Mboku is his name. He'll be there with a Japanese friend of his. You can't miss them.'

'I will.' Liar.

Afterwards Neil is gutted. Devastated, in fact. 'Dave, I fucked up. I'm sorry. I blew it. But what more can we do? The man simply won't engage. What do you have to do to get their attention?'

'Leave it with me, Neil. Something useful did come out of this morning: we now know a good place to stay in Dubai.'

Neil looks at me as if I'm mad, but it's true. And Happy and Nob will get to find out just how good it is.

I'M IN a smoker coming back from Italy. I'm too discreet to say where I've been or what I've been doing, suffice to say that 'bunga bunga' works for me. The flight back gives me time to reflect.

I like to think I have good instincts. I can generally smell a deal and know when something is worth pursuing and when it's not. I think media and sport will come good, and we'll make a lot of money, but in the meantime I need something else. I'm thinking food. Not regular food, but specifically, sugar.

I've never had a particularly sweet tooth, so I'm not in an ideal position to judge Big Sugar, but my uneducated view is that Big Sugar is as bad for humanity as Big Tobacco and Big Pharma, which is to say that we're conditioned almost from birth to consume far more of it than is good for us, and without regard for the consequences. I know all about addiction, and I'd say sugar is clearly addictive. And it doesn't just make us obese, it gives us cancer as well. Well, it's bound to if you have enough of it. Most things do.

My thinking started when I went to have a medical. Why did I bother? I never used to, although as a banker I was 'encouraged' to go every couple of years. No doubt the firm wanted to cover itself as a good employer, and they didn't want any bad surprises at an inconvenient stage in a deal. It was always a pain, because I had to dry out and leave the drugs alone for a month beforehand. I was nearly out of my mind by the time I got to sit in front of the doctor, and so of course my blood pressure was sky high, because I was off the fucking drugs. What did he expect?

But this time I went along to a new clinic off the Kings Road, a smart, high-end commercial operation specialising in corporate services for people in finance. Or maybe it's people with finance. Either way, it's a high-end commercial operation and reassuringly expensive.

I did it for Two Livers. That may sound odd, but she's in great shape and I'm . . . well, I guess I'm in pretty normal shape by the standards of the investment banking industry, which is to say I'm overweight (though not massively so), unfit, have a poor diet, drink far too much and indulge too frequently in substances best left alone.

I was subjected to half a day of blood tests and physical examinations. I was hooked up to high-tech machinery straight out of a science fiction movie, and even had a brain scan that can pick up frontal lobe tumours. Why frontal lobe tumours? Apparently frontal lobe tumours can result in disinhibition, behavioural disturbance and poor judgement. Enough said. At the end I sat down with the quack, who asked me what sort of report I was after.

'What sort? What do you mean?'

'Well, Mr Hart – is this report for insurance purposes? Or for a prospective employer?'

'It's for me. It's personal.'

'You mean . . . you want to know how you really are?'

'Of course. What did you think I wanted?'

'Well . . . we're a very thorough organisation. We have patients – we prefer to call them clients – who need all kinds of reports. For all kinds of different purposes.'

I get it. That's why they're so expensive. 'No, I just want the truth.'

He actually looked disappointed. If all I wanted was the truth, I could have gone elsewhere and paid half the price. He glanced down at his notes. 'Well, Mr Hart, subject to getting back some of the test results over the next day or two, I'd say you're in much better shape than you deserve to be. I put that down to your parents.'

'What do you mean? What have my parents got to do with this?'

'Mr Hart, if you want to live to a ripe old age, the best thing you can do is choose the right parents. You clearly did. You drink far too much, you test positive for things you shouldn't, you're unfit and, by clinical standards, you're mildly obese. But you'll probably live for a good few decades yet.'

'Is there anything you'd advise me to do to change my lifestyle? I mean anything realistic?'

'Nothing you'd be likely to do, no. Although you could always cut down on sugary foods.'

And bingo! A light went on in my head. We don't need less sugar. We need better sugar.

SO TODAY I'm seeing John Mills, the chief executive of International Sugar Corporation, the UK's largest and oldest sugar producer. His office is out towards Heathrow, in a thirties brick-built complex that would once have been impressive and state of the art, but now seems quaint. In fact a lot about this business seems quaintly out of date, which I'm sure helps them keep a low profile. That's all about to change.

Tom drops me at the main entrance, where an old-style commissionaire welcomes me, takes me inside and shows me to a seat in a waiting area. There are black-and-white photographs on the walls of well-dressed smiling workers in a dozen or more countries around the world. ISC is proud of its history and reputation. A truly great British company.

I'm not ready to go in yet, because I'm waiting for the rest of the team. DLR Strummer are sending two of the biggest lawyers in the firm, and I'm also waiting for . . . Two Livers!

She's joining me for this one, and it's going to be just like the old days. Grossbank bailed out ISC last year. They refinanced them in the middle of the credit crunch, when the bank they were going to deal with nearly went bust and pulled all its credit lines. They owe her one.

The legal team arrive and the firm has once again done me proud. These guys are huge. Put wires in their ears and they could work at the White House. If I didn't have such a massive ego I'd feel quite insignificant next to them.

Two Livers arrives a few minutes later. She's wearing a dark grey mid-length skirt and jacket by Valentino, sober yet sexy, and heels by Jimmy Choo. Did I say sober? I could undress her right now.

She gives me a peck on the cheek, I introduce her to the legal team and we all go upstairs to meet John Mills.

His office is small and ordinary. No rampaging egos here, just a few family photos on an otherwise neat and tidy desk. With the lawyers in the room, it feels positively tiny. He shows us to a small table in the corner of the office and helps push a couple of chairs round so we can all sit down. He's late fifties, stooped, balding, very polite and low key, an ISC lifer who started at the firm at sixteen and never went anywhere else. Now he's in charge.

Looking at him, I bet that when he started his mates thought him the man least likely to succeed. But he stayed and they didn't, and, just the same as in investment banking, the last man standing finds himself in charge. He's probably as surprised as the rest of them.

He clearly doesn't like the lawyers being present, probably wonders why they are here and possibly finds them quite scary. That's the point, John. You're meant to be scared. He's very polite with Two Livers, because he knows she saved him when he was in the shit, and you always stay on the right side of the bank.

So he offers us instant coffee and says how surprised he was by my call, but he's heard that I've been buying his shares in the market. Apparently he always likes to meet his shareholders. At least he did until today.

'Mr Mills, I won't beat about the bush. I'm here to talk about the harm done by your industry – not in a negative, critical sense, but in a positive one. I want to invest to put things right.'

He glances at Two Livers, but she's giving nothing away. Why is she here? He's an important client of hers, but presumably I am too. Is she here to broker a deal, and if so what kind of deal?

'Mr Hart, I'm not sure I follow you.'

'I'm talking about sugar. Big Sugar.'

'Oh, really? Mr Hart, you shouldn't believe everything you read in the papers. There's really no such thing as Big Sugar. And if there is, we're not part of it. We're a food solutions company.'

Food solutions? Yeah, right. And Heckler and Koch, who make the best sub-machine guns in the world, are in the business of pacification and conflict resolution.

'Mr Mills, I won't try to teach you your business. I'm sure you're aware of the medical research currently underway on the effects of sugar in our diet. I suspect you follow it closely.' He looks wary. Probably doesn't follow it at all until it's published – too busy running his company. 'You'll be aware that an avalanche of reports are due out this autumn. There'll be a ton of publicity. Most of it bad. In fact all of it bad.'

That bit has to be true. What's the point of publishing reports that don't scare us? You don't get funding by telling people they don't need to worry. Mills isn't saying anything. No doubt he wishes he had his chief scientific adviser with him – if he has one. I go on:

'Reports are going to show that we all consume far too much sugar. Highly processed sugar that isn't just associated with simple stuff like tooth decay and diabetes, heart disease, arteriosclerosis, mental illness, depression, senility, hypertension, hyperactivity in children, damage to the liver, pancreas and adrenal glands, and, of course, cancer. All that we know about. These reports are going to show a direct link to impotence as well.' OK, I made that one up. But he looks concerned and he's scribbling frantic notes at the end of the table. 'Your industry is heading for a fall. Sugar consumption is heading for a fall. You're facing a once-in-a-generation decline in demand. It's just around the corner and you need to do something about it now.'

I'm half expecting him to disagree with me. At least about impotence.

'What do you suggest, Mr Hart?'

Wow. He hasn't shown me the door. But then he couldn't, not with the bank sitting next to me.

'Mr Mills, do you ever take a walk late at night and find yourself looking up at the sky? Looking at the millions of stars in the universe?'

'Sometimes. It can make you feel quite insignificant.'

'Really?' Strange. Has the opposite effect on me. Makes me think that all those millions of stars are there for me, looking down on me, lighting my way. But I guess that's why I'm in global finance and he's in food solutions. 'Well, you must have noticed how some stars shine more brightly than the rest. So far, ISC has been one of those bright stars. But unless you get in now, ahead of the curve, and reposition this company, your star could fade and even disappear altogether. What we want to talk about, Mr Mills, is how you do that – with our help and finance.'

'What exactly did you have in mind, Mr Hart?'

'Call me Dave. Forget the substance, it's all about presentation. Ninety per cent of everything we ever do is about presentation. You need to produce a few new lines of product, probably less refined, less synthetic, and then market the hell out of them. Dazzle the customers and shame the competition. Become seen as the healthy alternative. With our money.'

He looks nonplussed. 'Oh . . . I thought you were going to say something different altogether.'

'Really? What was that?'

'Something about fair trade practices with the developing world. You know – buying cane sugar grown in poor countries rather than sugar beet grown in enormous, taxpayer-subsidised farms in Europe and North America. A lot of people have strong views about that.'

I make a sweeping gesture with my hand. 'We don't care about that.'

He seems a little surprised and looks across at Two Livers, who's said nothing so far but scribbles a note and passes it to me. I glance at it. She cares. Damn. I slip it into my pocket.

'No, you're right. We care enormously. We want to reinvent the supply chain completely. We have no interest in pandering to powerful lobbyists in Brussels and Washington acting on behalf of farmers' groups in the developed world. We want to support poor third world nations growing sugarcane. Sugarcane grows in the fresh air, it tastes better, it's a superior crop, it's even healthier. Sugar beet's a root crop. It grows in mud. Who wants to eat sugar that grows in mud?'

OK, it wasn't a vintage performance, and I let Two Livers come in and take it on after that. She'd actually prepared for the meeting, knew what she was talking about and had got the lawyers to draft an investment proposal, backed up with fresh loans from Grossbank.

She and I are like a jazz ensemble. When one of us fades, the other takes the lead. Except she didn't really fade, but ran with it all the way to the end, when we shook hands with John Mills and said our goodbyes. He looked surprisingly grateful, though I got the sense that more of it was directed at her than at me.

But still, we're a great team, and afterwards we said goodbye to the lawyers and she came back to the Ritz to celebrate. Now that's what I call a successful meeting.

'NEIL MORELAND on line three.'

Maria's voice pulls me out of a trance. I've been staring at my desk, fantasising about Two Livers and imagining ... Well, anyway, Neil's on line three and it's possible for you to have too much information.

'Neil? How are you? What's up?'

'Dave – I just had a call from Charles Merton.'

'Who?'

'Charles at MileHigh TV. That meeting didn't go as badly as we thought.'

'Really? What did he want?'

'He wants to get us back in. He wants to introduce us to his chairman and board of directors, and he says he's keen to get behind our project. He says he's going to recommend that MileHigh back it.'

'Amazing. So we did get his attention after all.' I try to sound surprised and excited, but I'm not. I'd be backing us if Happy Mboku and Nob had held me by my ankles from the balcony of my suite on the sixty-third floor of the Al Khalid in Dubai. Must have been quite a view, especially upside down.

'So what are the next steps?'

'I've agreed we'll meet him Tuesday afternoon. I'm emailing across detailed proposals and draft agreements. Do you want to join us? It's Tuesday at three.'

'No. I don't think I could stand being in the same room as that wanker twice in one lifetime. But I'll send someone. I think I'll send Happy. And maybe Nob too, if he's free.'

GOOD PERFORMANCE deserves recognition. I've been holding off from doing this for a while, but I think the team deserve a night out.

We're going to Horrors on Greek Street, a nightclub come pick-up joint, and I'm going to burn the corporate plastic to give everyone some R & R. It's true that I haven't invited Maria, and actually went to some lengths in the office to hide from her what we were planning. I'm sure I failed completely, but that's not the point. This is not a large firm with PC thought police, and I don't have to live in fear of employment tribunals – not that I ever did. We can recognise that we employ a bunch of guys who will bond together and be better motivated by getting pissed and shagging, while at the same time valuing the contribution of Maria, who gets a million pound bonus at year end if she's lasted the course. The guys get laid, she gets paid. Who's smarter? I wouldn't like to say. I simply observe that people are different.

There are twelve of us, and I suppose we don't look like your average investment bankers. When we arrive, the guys on the door start speaking into their headsets and, within moments, reinforcements arrive. And then the manager appears. He's mid-fifties, square build with close-cropped white hair and a bushy moustache. I'm guessing he didn't get to be manager by being good in the accounts department.

'Hello – Dave Hart. I called yesterday. Twelve of us for an office party. A VIP party.' I unpeel some fifties and he stares at us. They all stare at us. 'It's OK, we've just come to have a good time.' I think they thought another gang were moving in on them. 'We're traders. City traders. We run a hedge fund.'

'You run a hedge fund? Sure you do.'

He nods slowly and stares as we check our coats in and go downstairs. Maybe he recognises some of the team from a previous life? Maybe they recognise him? For some reason, I'm the only one smiling.

Downstairs we have two large tables in a separately cordoned-off 'VIP' area next to the dance floor, where we get to pay double the already very high prices for our drinks. I order champagne, which I don't think anyone will drink except me, several rounds of beer, which I know will go down well, and tell the manager to bring on the girls.

The dance floor fills with several dozen beautiful creatures from all over the world, dressed in short skirts and low-cut tops, who do their moves and smile at us, hoping to be selected to make our work outing the success we all intend it to be.

I grin at the team. 'No more than two each.'

Our tables are soon packed, more chairs are brought, but even so we have to accommodate a lot of girls on our laps, and space is so short that a couple have to be directed to go underneath the table because there just isn't enough space around it. And, of course, the girls all order drinks – champagne, which must be a standing instruction from the club.

I look around at the other tables, the non-VIP ones, and can tell we're getting a lot of ugly looks. Who do we think we are, coming in here, taking the best seats next to the dance floor, showing off with our fancy drinks orders, and then getting all the best girls? And just what is going on underneath the table? Nothing's supposed to happen on the premises. This is London. There are discreet hotels around the corner for that sort of thing.

I like pissing people off. Who do they think they are, these little people with small expense accounts whose firms won't sign off the kind of excess we can get away with? We can do anything we want. Well, almost.

I look across, catch the eye of a couple of scowling middle-aged men and raise my champagne glass. 'Cheers, chaps.'

'Fuck you.'

What did he just say? I look again. He's mid-forties, big, shaven-headed and would have been tough once upon a time, but now he's running to fat. He's wearing a cheap ready-made suit and a tie that might even be polyester. He's drinking beer, and he doesn't have a girl on his lap or under his table. His friend is taller and leaner and looks away, not wanting to get involved.

'Not got a girl? Want one of ours?' I say it as if I'm being generous. 'Go on – help yourself. We've got plenty.' I know I'm winding him up, but what's wrong with a little exuberance from time to time?

But when he gets up from his table and walks over to

ours, I wonder if I've gone too far. I hold out my hand.

'Dave Hart. And this is my team.'

The girl sitting next to me, a twenty-one-year-old from Estonia whose name I keep forgetting, senses trouble and slips away to the ladies' room. He leans forward and jabs me in the chest.

'I don't give a fuck who you are. As far as I'm concerned, you're just a rich wanker.'

I push my chair back just far enough from the table for him to get sight of the blonde head bobbing up and down in my lap.

'I'm not a wanker. No need. See?'

For some reason this doesn't have the effect I intend. Instead of being impressed by my awesomeness, he's incensed and grabs a beer bottle from the table – one of our beer bottles – and holds it like a weapon.

Which is when a large Japanese hand picks up another bottle and I find myself sitting in semi darkness as Nob steps between Mr Angry and me, blocking out most of the light.

Mr Angry's still mad at me and stands his ground. 'This is between me and him. Nothing to do with you. I'm not looking for trouble. This is private.'

Nob says nothing, just raises the beer bottle he's picked up and smashes it over his own head, shattering it and spraying glass and beer everywhere. Mr Angry takes a step back, still holding the bottle he picked up earlier. Somebody turns the music off and in the sudden silence all eyes are on him. He looks around, feeling the pressure . . . and slams the bottle against his own head. Oddly, it doesn't smash, just makes a thunking noise. He sways, his eyes roll upwards, and he staggers back a step and topples over onto the floor, unconscious. I guess it's all a matter of technique. His friend rushes forward and tries to drag him back to their table, but the bouncers have arrived and the pair of them are shown the door. Or at least his friend is shown the door. Mr Angry is carried out. I half expect similar trouble, but they leave us alone.

Well, you would, wouldn't you?

I can't remember when we finished, but I do remember Sly and Timur helping me out to a cab, my trousers falling down, my shirt undone, my legs somehow not obeying orders, and my body covered in lipstick marks that I'd discover the following morning … always a helpful reminder of what you were up to the previous evening.

WELL, THAT was a success.

Tom's driving me to a meeting with some private bankers who want to invest in the fund. That's right. They're asking me now. And they're grateful when I find time for them. We've done a second closing that takes us through the thirty billion level. That's thirty billion with a two per cent management fee and twenty per cent of any upside over ten per cent a year. Real money.

This is how I like it. If I keep going like this, I could even buy Grossbank.

The private bankers would have come to me, but I don't want them to see the team in their present condition, so I'm even more accommodating than they could possibly have hoped.

Tom has a twinkle in his eye. 'Good night last night?'

'Not sure I remember.'

The people I'm meeting are based, of all places, in Canary Wharf, which means we have to brave the traffic all the way from the West End and sit and fume at all the wasted time while I start to sweat out last night's alcohol and observe the slow onset of a dull ache in the centre of my brain and a general slowing down of my responses and ability to think.

I'd like to say I'm beyond hangovers. There was a time when I was much younger when I really didn't seem to get them. I'd drink huge quantities, watch everyone else getting pissed and acting foolishly, and pick my moment to take whatever advantage I was seeking, particularly if they were young and cute and female. And then I started to worry. I could drink and drink and nothing would happen at all, except that I'd feel like shit the next day. Luckily that was when I discovered drugs.

I relax into my seat and close my eyes, and could easily drift off into a deep sleep, hoping the journey will never come to an end and that I'll wake up with my energy restored, ready to party once more. Unfortunately, though, Tom knowing London better than most cabbies, we get there quickly and on time, and I find myself reporting to reception and being shown into a meeting room.

Three of them come in, smartly dressed young women, two blondes and a brunette, in conservative business suits, and curiously, all three of them are wearing glasses and have their long hair rather severely tied up. They're enthusiastic, very excited to meet me and full of compliments about the performance of the fund: the clever play with conglomerates, the daring moves in the mining sector, the visionary reinvention of the fund management business.

And as they talk, they let their hair down. Literally. And then they take their glasses off, showing just how cute they are. One of them, with bright red lipstick, starts sucking the end of the pen she's brought to take notes. And then the one at the end of the table starts unbuttoning her blouse. Is this for real? It can't be. I know I'm a sex god, superhuman, a finance rock star, and I can understand why beautiful young women might fall for me, but it does seem a little odd in a private banking meeting. I pinch myself. Could I still be asleep in the back of Tom's car, day-dreaming? Nah, because then the real action starts as they get up and all the clothes start coming off. In no time they're down to their lingerie, classic black stockings and suspenders, the bras come off and their hands are all over me.

Which is when the meeting room door opens and a familiar voice calls out, 'Surprise!'

Fuck. Shit. This is not fair. I'm not in great shape today. My brain is not working properly. I have one of those awful 'Where am I? Who am I?' moments. I look to my left and there's Dan Harriman, with a grin as wide as a double-decker bus.

Dan and I have history together. We worked as colleagues and competitors in the City, we were drinking buddies, shagging buddies and fellow miscreants. Together we misbehaved massively and put a lot of miles on the clock. He even had a thing going with Two Livers at one point, which stretched our friendship a little far.

But now Dan must be about fifty and wears his years badly. Fat, balding, florid, permanently puffing and perspiring, he's the living embodiment of a government health warning on the perils of excess. Fifty going on sixty.

But he knows how to live.

I stand up, disentangling myself from the girls, and he gives me a bear hug.

'How are you, Dave? You don't write, you don't call. Being dead was a good excuse, but you've been back ages now.'

'I'm good, Dan. Big night last night, but I'm good. And you're right. I should have been in touch. But things have just been . . . crazy.'

We talk about old times, the girls get busy working their magic, and thanks be to God for whoever invented Viagra. Dan is the most hospitable of hosts, and it would have been churlish of me not to take full advantage. Afterwards, when they've gone and we're slumped on the sofa in the conference room, he tells me what he's up to.

'Private banking. It's the next big thing, Dave. There's so much money in the world. So many rich people. And they're just like us. They want service. All kinds of service. And they find it hard at most firms to get the kind of special services they want, if you know what I mean. It's a huge opportunity. Especially for washed-up old has-beens like me, who can't get a job at a proper firm anymore.'

Dan used to run equities at Hardman Stoney – a big job. But now I look at him closely, at the lined face, the latticework of little red veins on the end of his nose, the perspiration running down his forehead from the exertions he just put himself through with what were clearly a very well-briefed team of professionals, and I see what I might have become – or might yet if I don't achieve what I intend with Two Livers. Dan has had two divorces, probably slept with more women than I have, certainly drinks more and, I'm guessing, has done more drugs. He's a living pharmaceutical miracle. Eat your heart out, Keith Richards.

But it's come at a cost. He's fallen off the career ladder and ended up at a private banking firm, earning a living supplying hookers and drugs to rich people. On reflection, it's probably a lot more fun than running equities at Hardman Stoney, and there's definitely more of a long-term future in it. As long as he doesn't get caught. But that applies to most of the things we do.

I pick up my jacket, which is lying in a heap on the floor where it was discarded in my earlier haste to get fully involved in the action, and I take a couple of Cohibas from the inside pocket and offer him one.

'Can't. Not in here.' He points at a smoke detector in the ceiling.

'Really? What kind of firm is this? Lucky they don't have CCTV in the meeting rooms.'

'Smoking's against the law. Management won't allow it.'

'But hookers are OK?'

'They're more understanding about that.'

'Dan, what are you doing here?'

'I didn't have much choice. I was knifed in the back at Hardman Stoney and I needed to make money. Where am I supposed to get money from? The fairies don't bring it.'

'I have money.'

'So I heard.'

'Well, you can have it too. Some of it anyway. Come to us. You're old enough to be our chairman.'

'Why do you need a chairman?'

'We don't. No one needs a chairman. You'd be perfect.'

'What does it pay?'

'Whatever you want.'

'You're taking the piss.'

'Try me.'

SO NOW we have a chairman. Maria disapproves, and her instincts are usually good, because Dan has a certain reputation – as if I don't. But the trading team like him, because he goes into the dealing room every day and orders lunch with them, and probably other things as well, and even the investment committee like him, because he chairs our meetings particularly efficiently, so that the formal business of the day is rapidly concluded and we can all adjourn to somewhere more interesting, which he's happy to organise. He gets into the office first in the morning and often leaves last. In fact he's putting in so many hours I can't even work out myself what he's doing. Most chairmen understand they don't actually have to work – they're just a figurehead. OK, so quite often they're an expensive figurehead, but all the best ornaments cost money.

When I meet Two Livers for a martini, she asks why I hired him.

'Was it pity?'

'Love.'

'Love? What do you mean?'

'He's a mate. Someone I can trust. And in this business that's all you have. Your mates.' It's true. In the Square Mile the word 'colleague' can cover a multitude of evils.

She nods. 'I understand. You know he has a bad reputation?'

'For drink? Or drugs? Or women? Or all of the above?'

'For business. He got fired from Hardman Stoney.'

'Who cares? Good people get fired all the time in our business. Your face doesn't fit, you get fired. You don't sing the corporate song loud enough, you get fired. You don't ask brown-nose questions at a town hall with the chairman, you get fired. You show some character, you get fired. You're just in the wrong place at the wrong time, and you're toast. All roads lead to hell. These days the best people get fired.'

'Not if they produce. He stopped producing.'

'Producing what? He spent a lifetime on the trading floor pushing stocks to big investors, writing tickets, getting bored. Same old, same old. You can't do that forever.'

'OK, but I don't think that's what got him fired. Dave, I heard he became unreliable.'

'What does that mean? We're all unreliable. Well, some of us are, anyway. The males who work around here, which just happens to be most of us.' I'm feeling angry, defensive, even like I'm getting pissed off with her, which I don't want because I'm meant to be selling.

She picks up her glass and drains it in one. Damn, she's good. 'I'd better go. Think about what I said. And don't get caught short.' She gets up to leave.

Damn. Fuck. Shit. This is not meant to be happening. A couple of martinis – well, a couple for me, she might have three or four – and then on to dinner and eventually bed. That was the plan. Fuck Dan Harriman.

'OK, I'll fire him. Consider it done. He's gone. He'll be taken out and shot first thing tomorrow. I'll do it myself. *Sayonara.*' I look up at her hopefully, puppy-like, pathetic.

'Don't.' She holds up a hand and looks away. A sigh. She's pissed off. Exasperated. The last thing I wanted. 'Dave, just be Dave Hart. Listen to what I said. Think about it. I said it for a reason.'

'OK, got it.'

'And remember it.'

I tap the side of my head. 'Goldfish brain. Three-second memory. But I'll write it down.' I reach for a napkin, get a pen from my jacket pocket and write 'Fire Dan' in large letters.

This at least gets a laugh, but she doesn't change her

mind and gives me a brief kiss – on the lips – and leaves.

Fuck Dan Harriman.

I'M GOING to the Treasury again. This time I've actually got an appointment to see the minister – the new one, who took over from Lord Bigmann – and this time I have a fully worked-up proposal that doesn't involve the NHS.

The new minister is a 'real' politician, one who's never done anything else, and so he isn't a patch on his predecessor. Bigmann finally crashed and burned in business as well as everything else. It seems the word went out in the scrap metal industry that his firm was not to be trusted. Funny how these things spread. All of a sudden no one wanted to do business with him anymore. And then he was arrested and charged with tax evasion. He only spent one night in prison before being bailed, but apparently it was a 'slopping out' jail, where the inmates get to use a bucket in their cells if they're caught short in the night. As a former politician, the good lord made too tempting a target for a golden shower in the morning. Life's a bitch.

So I'm sitting opposite Jim Bradman, a thirty-eight-year-old Lib Dem idealist who thinks that bankers' bonuses are egregious, that the City needs reform and that it's all so terribly unfair that bankers fucked up and ordinary people had to bail them out. Get real, pal. That's what ordinary people are for. And that's why we need so many of them. It's all those little guys who carry the rest of us – including the politicians who tell them what to do, take half their earnings away and spend it badly on crappy things we'd be better off buying for ourselves.

I thought about wearing sandals today as a sign of respect, but they wouldn't have gone with my suit, so I chose slip-on shoes with a side buckle by Fratelli Rossetti instead of lace-ups. I think slip-ons are more Lib Dem.

I've come alone and empty-handed, which rather throws him, because he was warned about the last meeting and has a line-up of eight on his side of the table. And someone did a coffee run and there are takeaway cups from Starbucks lined up in military ranks at one end of the table, as well as a box of Krispy Kreme doughnuts.

Village People is there again and makes a point of offering me a coffee.

'Thank you, that's very kind. Can I get a skinny hazelnut latte with a shot?'

He looks cluelessly at the rows of coffee cups, then at one of his colleagues, a young guy with a high forehead, long, delicate fingers and the kind of cerebral air of someone with a first in economics from Cambridge who'll go far at the Treasury but will never be trusted with a coffee order again.

I can sense the bewilderment, so I decide to let Village People off the hook and turn to the coffee boy and speak slowly.

'Don't worry. Just let me have a grande, two-pump vanilla, non-fat, extra hot latte.'

He looks helplessly at his boss. The minister clears his throat.

'Mr Hart – I think we only have a simple selection here. Would you like any of these?'

'Of course, minister. Regular black filter will be fine.'

The young guy looks relieved as he passes me a coffee. 'Doughnut, Mr Hart?'

He's about to open the box, so I get my order in quickly.

'Sure. Cinnamon apple and butterscotch fudge.'

He looks crestfallen.

'OK, lemon meringue pie?'

He shakes his head.

'Chocolate iced with sprinkles?'

'Yes!' He opens the box and produces one with a flourish. I hold my hand up and we high five. I turn to the minister and I'm about to high five with him, but I get a glare from Village People and sit down instead. Bonding moments are great, but we have to respect the dignity of office.

I can tell that for the Treasury team this is like a work outing. Coffee and doughnuts with the minister, and all they have to do is listen to me for half an hour.

'So, Mr Hart, a sad day.'

As an opening ministerial gambit, it strikes me as a little odd.

'I'm sorry, minister?'

'You haven't heard about my predecessor?'

'Er . . . no. I don't think so.'

'The papers will have it soon if they haven't got it already. He took his own life last night.'

'Lord Bigmann? Really?' No time for subterfuge now. I'm genuinely shocked. A smart old fucker like that should have been able to bounce back from anything.

'I'm afraid so.' Then he gives me an oddly meaningful stare. 'At least we think he did. He jumped off Blackfriars Bridge.'

The canny old sod. I wonder if he knows Bang Bang Lee. I sit back in my chair and have to take a moment to compose myself. 'A terrible way to go.'

'Apparently. Of course . . . he'd been under a lot of pressure.'

All the heads around the table nod in agreement.

'I agree, minister. A lot of pressure.'

'Everything seemed to go wrong for him in such a short space of time . . . just after your meeting with him, Mr Hart.'

I'm not sure where this is going, but I don't like it. 'Things sometimes happen like that, minister. And for politicians these days, well, the media expect them to be whiter than white. And Lord Bigmann had . . . the odd skeleton in his closet.'

Foolish bastard had a whole graveyard full of them. Live dangerously if you must, but don't go into politics and be careful who you piss off.

The minister clears his throat, raises his eyebrows in a friendly, half-mocking way and looks at me expectantly. 'So, Mr Hart – you have something you want to say to us?'

This time I do it properly. I emailed Two Livers the bullet points yesterday evening, and overnight she completely rewrote them, reordered them and added half a dozen I hadn't thought of, but most importantly she offered a financing package from Grossbank.

So I argue persuasively, using her words, for the government to bundle up its real-estate assets, taking them off the balance sheet, moving them into a property company in which it would retain a controlling stake but which it could sell down and privatise whenever it wanted to, and which would capture and harness a whole lot of private sector finance on a scale government never managed to in the past. It's actually a good piece of advice, soundly argued and in the national interest. Obviously the devil would be in the detail, but it sounds like a runner. The minister looks at me curiously.

'I can see the fees and the commercial potential, Mr Hart, but what's really in this for you?'

They're all listening now. Why did I come back to the Treasury? Why not roll with the punches, walk away and focus on something easier and more interesting than dealing with government?

'I'm stubborn, minister. And a bad loser.'

He nods. 'My wife says the same thing about me, Mr Hart. Are you married?'

'Not yet, minister. I tried it once and it didn't work. But I haven't given up. I never do.'

AS A man, what do I have to offer? What does any man have to offer? These days, not a lot. If a woman is beautiful, intelligent and successful, why fuck up her life by involving a man in it? If she wants to get laid, she can do that via the internet the same way we can. If she wants a sperm donor, she can get that too. If she doesn't need us for the money – and most do – we really don't serve much purpose.

Get a grip, Hart. I'm super successful, albeit in a criminally devious, insane kind of way. I know my way around London, I understand markets and I can navigate a wine list. I've done a lot of things, some of which I could even tell her about. And a woman can feel safe with me – as long as I have my six foot five inch sumo wrestler with me. I'm quite a package.

Of course I won't be faithful, but who is? And I'll get pissed and be out of my mind on chemicals from time to time, but that's normal these days, at least among successful people. Assuming I haven't suffered damage I don't know about, I can father children. I can certainly provide for children. Look what I provide for Samantha. It all adds up to a pretty compelling case, and if I wanted a classic Chelsea trophy wife, I could get one.

The problem is I want Two Livers. And I think I want her more than she wants me. If she really wants me at all.

I'm still in this daze when the phone on my desk buzzes. It's Maria. 'Mr Hart, I have Mr Lee for you on line two.'

What does Bang Bang want? Our performance figures are great, we're really motoring, and we're not due to meet for another month. Probably wants to congratulate me again.

'Bang Bang. How are you?'

'I'm not good, Dave. Not good at all. We need to talk.' There's no friendliness, no banter, just a coded reference to a pre-agreed time and place where we can meet. He hangs up.

Shit. What just happened? I look out at the trading floor and Dan Harriman catches my eye. I still haven't fired him. It's eleven in the morning and he's pissed. He looks up and raises a bottle in my direction. It's Krug. He's drinking Krug from the bottle at eleven in the morning. Normally it wouldn't bother me. Normally I might even go and join him, but today I have a bad feeling. Dan's always hanging around, and I still can't work out what he does. He shouldn't really need to come in at all, except for board meetings. Maybe he doesn't have anywhere else to go. Some fucking chairman he turned out to be.

IT'S 6 p.m. and Bang Bang is sitting in a private booth in a wine bar off Fleet Street. When I first come in, I think it must be doing fantastic trade with the Chinese. The guys behind the bar are Chinese, the customers sitting and standing at the bar all seem to be Chinese, the people in the booths are Chinese. And they're all youngish men of a similar age, wearing smart business suits, white shirts, dark ties and sunglasses. Absolutely no women at all. For a moment I wonder if Bang Bang's brought me to a Chinese gay bar. Some places do get a reputation as a cool place for particular nationalities to hang out, but as I look around the penny drops. Everyone here works for Bang Bang. They're all his guys. Normally that would make me feel secure, but tonight it troubles me.

When I sit down he stares impassively at me. He's distant, not hostile, but there's certainly no warmth in the air tonight. Where's the love, Bang Bang? Where's the friendship? Where's a drink? We're in a fucking bar, for Christ's sake.

'Dave, we have a problem.'

'Problem? Bang Bang, the only problem we have is that we're too successful. We're up forty per cent on paper and, at this rate, give me a few months and we'll double our money. We'll double your money. We're doing well, Bang Bang. Very well indeed. Show me anyone else whose performance is even close to ours.'

'Dave, someone in our organisation has attracted the attention of . . . certain government departments. People we don't want looking into our business are now doing so.'

I'm stunned. This isn't what I was expecting at all. 'Impossible. Everyone on the team is vetted. Between us we know all of them and they're all reliable. What you're saying just doesn't stack up.'

'Dave, some things I know. I don't know who . . . yet. But someone on the team is not reliable.' He shrugs. 'Perhaps we should just kill them all.'

What? My team? My boys? I try not to sound desperate. 'Bang Bang, they're good guys. Trust me on this. I know them, I like them, I'm sure we can count on them.'

'All of them?'

'All of them.'

'Dave, I hope you're not becoming sentimental. In business, you can't become too attached to people. Sometimes it's good to change . . . to upgrade or refresh the team.'

'Upgrade or refresh? Bang Bang you're talking black bagging. You want to get rid of them.'

He shrugs. 'If black bagging is what investment bankers do, we can put them in black bags. Afterwards.'

'No, you don't understand. I meant firing them. Not with guns. Telling them to clear their desks and put their personal possessions in a black bag.'

'That's not what I had in mind, Dave.' Oh, Christ. This is starting to feel like defeat from the jaws of victory. I have to make one final plea. 'Not this team, Bang Bang. Trust me on this. They're really good. I love them, and we work really well together.'

He frowns. 'Dave, I'm going to take some steps to find out how much of what we're doing has leaked to people who really don't need to know about it. And who is the source of the leak. And then, Dave . . . we have to take decisive action.'

HOW DID it come to this? All I wanted to do was make a few more billion, turn the global economy around and get the girl. And, if I'm honest – which I rarely am and least of all when I start a sentence by mentioning it – I'd forget about the rest if I could just have the girl.

But now unspecified government departments are looking into my operation, someone on the team can't be trusted and Bang Bang's talking about killing people.

Investment banking was never meant to be like this. In the past I took it for granted that no one on any of my teams could ever be trusted – we were bankers, and that really said it all. But there's something about criminals that's so much more honourable. Guys like Happy and Nob and Sly and Timur know their place in the hierarchy, stick to their word and sometimes take great risks. Holding someone by his ankles from the top of a skyscraper in Dubai requires nerve. What if you slipped and dropped them by mistake? But they didn't. These guys are good, and I like being around them. I feel . . . tribal about them in a way I never could about investment banking colleagues.

I need to talk to someone, which is weird. I never need to talk to anyone. Why would I? No one else is Dave Hart, so how could anyone else ever have insights and suggestions that compare with mine? But this time there is someone.

I call Two Livers, and for once I get straight through and she agrees to meet at the Dorchester. It's the launch event for MileHigh TV's new joint venture with Sir Neil Moreland – a whole range of new channels aimed at track and field events, swimming, sailing, cycling and a bunch of other things I never do.

When I get there she's got a quiet table in the bar where we can speak without being overheard. She has a bottle of Cristal on ice, two glasses, and she's wearing a pink satin mini dress by Dolce and Gabbana with gladiator sandals that always make me wish she wasn't wearing anything else.

'You're late. I'm on the second bottle.'

How does she do it and still look beautiful? I apologise and lean forward, strangely uncertain how to kiss her.

'Come here, stupid,' she says and puts her hand on the side of my face to steer my lips firmly towards hers. I sit down and a waiter appears to pour me a glass of champagne. I can smell her scent, I can almost taste her, and I totally, utterly want her. I want to possess her body, to run my hands and lips and tongue all over it, and then I want to make love to her. Lust? Base instinct? Crude physical vulgarity? Sure. All of the above.

'So what's up, Dave?'

She's the one woman in the world who merits total honesty. All the rest I'd lie to. It's not that I put her in a different moral category, simply that she'd see through me in an instant, so what's the point?

'I'm in the shit.'

'I know.'

'You know? How?'

'Why else would you call me like this? How bad is it?'

'Really bad. There's something you should know . . .'

And so I tell her. Everything. She listens, nods, takes it in, asks the odd smart question, but on the whole doesn't interrupt or even seem unduly shocked. Is she really a woman? If I didn't know it before, I know it now. I've truly struck gold with this girl.

'Dave, it's Dan Harriman.'

'What? What do you mean?'

'Dan's been in trouble. I don't know what kind, but trouble. When he moved into private banking, it wasn't because he fancied a career change. Hardman Stoney finally got fed up with him – he went too far with the drink or the drugs or the hookers, or more likely something really serious that they don't allow for in the employee code of conduct.'

'But . . . Dan was senior. And a big producer. The employee code of conduct isn't for senior people.'

'This time it was. He did something really bad.'

'Donkeys? Children? Arms smuggling? Is he a terrorist?'

'I've no idea. But there was talk that he could have been looking at something much more serious than getting fired. There were rumours of criminal charges. Serious ones. And then . . . nothing happened. Nothing at all. Dan shows up as a private banker catering to all kinds of dodgy clients in interesting parts of the world. Private bankers are meant to be discreet, but everyone has their price. Perhaps Dan's price was his freedom.'

'You mean . . . he's a snitch?'

She throws her head back and laughs. 'That's exactly what I mean. Not the word I was going to use, but yes. I tried to warn you . . .'

'I know. And I made him chairman. The team love him. He gets pissed with them every day, he's in touch with some amazing dealers and he knows every club in town. He knows places I'd never even heard of.'

'But he's your leak. Don't be surprised if the size and success of the Salvation Fund attracted too much attention and the whole thing with Dan was a set-up.'

'You mean the police could do that?'

'Are you kidding?' She laughs again. 'No. This is someone else. Someone a little more serious.'

'If Bang Bang finds out about Dan, he'll kill him.'

'Dave, if I'm right about this, you might kill him yourself.'

I'm staring across the table at her and once again we have this amazing eye contact thing going – staring at each other, observing the tiniest movements, a kind of exquisite prelude to actual physical foreplay – when someone shouts across the bar. I turn and look. Fuck. It's Neil Moreland.

'Dave, Laura – how are you both? Dave, I had no idea

you were coming tonight. Your office said you couldn't make it.'

Make it? Me? I'm not sure if I'll make it either. But I'll bloody well try.

ALL INVESTMENT bankers are paranoid. It's the combination of high risk and high reward, coupled with short-time horizons and intense peer group rivalry. It's been said that it cruelly exposes the fault lines in human nature. There are a lot of fault lines running through the Square Mile.

But my natural paranoia is even worse now. I keep imagining – or are they real? – people following me wherever I go. I fancy that I can hear clicks on my telephone in the office, and I no longer trust my mobile or my email. I've started looking at people differently, wondering if the guy who sells me my newspaper is talking into a hidden microphone tucked behind his lapel, or if my 'therapist' at the high-end massage parlour I sometimes pop out to during the day has a hidden camera behind the shelves of aromatherapy oils that she so skilfully works into the more delicate parts of my body. It saps the will, and it's not sustainable.

I also look differently at Dan Harriman, and I think he can tell. I'm a heartbeat away from firing him, and only thoughts of old times get in the way. I no longer let him into my office without someone else present, and I don't tell him anything about the business, even though he's chairman. On reflection, that's probably a good way of dealing with all chairmen. Maybe I should have started sooner.

And then, of course, I have to push my luck. I have an

idea. A really good idea. I want to buy farmland in Africa. Forget the Gulf states and their food security agenda. Think Europe and America in the face of changing consumption patterns in China, India and elsewhere in Asia. We could soon need our own food security strategy. And it would sell well to investors, because we could dress it up in aid and development clothing, liberally sprinkled with the historical ties of the Commonwealth. I'm sure it's a winner, and I need to look some stuff up, write it down and collect my thoughts.

So although it's two in the morning I take a cab to the office. The lights are on and the alarm hasn't been set, but there's nothing strange in that. Probably some of the team are up here drinking or shagging or doing other stuff they shouldn't.

So when the lift doors open and I step out into the dealing room I'm a little shocked to see half a dozen guys I don't recognise wearing dark clothing and carrying toolkits. They've taken apart some of the computers and the telephones and various techie bits and pieces are all over the desks and the floor. They don't even pause, just carry on working, ignoring me. Why aren't they scared? Whoever was on lookout duty seems to have fucked up. I turn to the lift doors and jam my foot in between them before they can close, and then reach out for the fire alarm. Fuck this. Whoever these guys are, they can explain to the fire brigade.

But then a fat, chubby hand grabs my wrist, and I turn to see a face I do recognise.

'Dan, you fat wanker. What the fuck do you think you're doing?'

He's sweating, and his lips are wet and he smells of stale alcohol as he steps uncomfortably close to me.

'I'm saving my skin. And yours if you're smart.'

'You bastard. Who are these people?'

'Let's just say . . . they work for the government.'

'Government? Which government? Ours? How do you know?'

The other guys in the room are still working, silently going about their tasks with focussed concentration, as if we're not actually here.

'Mr Hart. We heard you were on your way. We were waiting for you.'

It's a commanding, very British voice, with a slight air of contempt. Contempt? For me? You must be kidding, pal. I bet I make more in a week than you make in a year.

A tall, fair-haired man in a pair of black overalls comes out of my office – *my* office! – and walks across to us. He removes a black leather glove and holds his hand out. 'A pleasure finally to meet you, Mr Hart.'

My hand stays resolutely where it is. 'You have the advantage over me. I don't know who I'm talking to.'

He drops his hand to his side. 'You don't need to.'

I'm not a man of violence at all. Violence is something best left to people who are good at it. But I really feel like smacking him in the mouth. Only he looks 'useful' in a way I've recognised before, and I think he'd spin me round, pin me to the ground and generally hurt and humiliate me before my fist got anywhere near his jaw.

'What are you doing here?'

'We're learning, Mr Hart. Learning about you and your operation. And if you don't mind me saying, what you've done here is fascinating. We're impressed. And we don't impress easily.'

This is surreal. I look at Dan. He's embarrassed,

uncomfortable and wretched. But he's got the look in his eye of someone who's used to that.

'What have they got on you, Dan? We were mates.'

He looks away. 'You don't want to know.'

I turn back to blondie, the steely-eyed killer. 'What next?'

'We weren't planning to talk to you quite yet. So for now you can go.'

'What? Go?'

'That's right. Unless you want to stay here and get on with your work? We won't be long.' He turns to his guys. 'Another thirty minutes?' They nod and give him the thumbs up. 'Don't try to leave the country, Mr Hart. We know where you are at all times. And we know who matters to you. You don't want to hurt anyone, do you, Mr Hart?'

Damn. Do they know about her? Fucking Harriman must have told them. Investment banking was never meant to be like this. 'I . . . I've got a few things to do.'

'That's fine. Go ahead.'

Go ahead? In my own fucking office? Who does this guy think he is? Just because I'm recycling billions of dollars in drug money into the legitimate economy, he thinks he can tell me what to do in my own office!

'Fuck you, pal.'

Who said that? Shit, it was me! And as I say it, I bring my foot up and kick him hard between the legs. Dan looks uncertain what to do and, with whatever little physical strength I have, I push him onto the steely-eyed killer, who is momentarily doubled up, and run flat out for the door to the fire escape, throwing it open and hitting the fire alarm button as I do so. I've never been here before, and find myself in a concrete stairwell with steps going down to the bottom of the building. I fly down the first flight, nearly tripping over myself in my haste, and just as I'm about to turn and head down to the next floor, a dark figure steps out from a doorway and something hard stops me in my tracks. I can feel the concrete floor against my cheek, my eyes won't focus and I happily slide into unconsciousness with that delicious escaping feeling that I last got from an opium pipe.

I THINK I'm dreaming. Two Livers is leaning over me, wearing what looks like a Cavallaro silk blouse, strategically unbuttoned at the top, bra-less and breathing hard. She must have rushed to my bedside, and the effect is startling. My head hurts, but I find myself wondering if I could reach out and tear her blouse open and pull her on top of me without doing myself permanent damage.

'Where am I?'

'You're at St Thomas's. They brought you here for a brain scan. There was a problem at the office. You were there at two in the morning. No one knows what you were doing. The fire alarm went off and you fell down the fire escape stairs. Dan Harriman called me. How do you feel?'

'Crap.' I look around the hospital room and put my finger to my lips. She nods. 'I need to get out of here.'

The hospital don't want to discharge me. I'm suffering from concussion. I need to take it easy and they want to keep me under observation – or at least someone does – for a day or so more. Fortunately Two Livers is not to be trifled with. The ward sister, a heavyweight Irishwoman who probably sees herself as an immovable object, suddenly learns what it's like to meet an irresistible force. We're leaving and not even physical violence will stop us, not that they'd try once they see the look on Two Livers' face. Tom is waiting outside and we head back to her place in Mayfair. Well, that's where she says we're going. We peel off down a narrow side street and I wonder what shortcut Tom's discovered to get there, when we suddenly stop and she opens the door, pulls me out and waves Tom on. We duck back inside an alleyway and watch as an unmarked white van with two men in the front swings past us on the tail of Tom's Merc.

'Where are we going?' My head hurts and I'm finding it hard to think straight.

'Somewhere safe. If there is a safe place for us now.'

'Us? Yeeeehaaaaa! I don't care where it is, as long as we're together.' I go to kiss her and she pushes me away.

'Don't get ahead of yourself.'

Another white van pulls up and we get in through a sliding door in the side. I look at the driver and it's Happy. He glances back at us and gives a big wide grin. That's three this year.

I turn to Two Livers. 'Is someone going to tell me where we're going?'

She shakes her head. 'Not yet. It involves a boat, a plane and another boat. And then swimming costumes and sunnies, possibly for quite a while.'

'You mean we're doing a runner? Getting out of town?' She nods. I shake my head, even though it hurts. 'No, not yet. We can't. If we do a runner now, we'll have everyone after us. Bang Bang and Rom, Dan's friends, the whole world. We have to be smarter than that.'

'So what do you suggest?'

My head still hurts and I can tell I'm not on the top of my game, but I smile reassuringly. 'I've got a plan.'

IT'S NIGHT-TIME, and I'm hiding in the bushes outside a farm cottage in Oxfordshire, feeling slightly ridiculous.

Investment bankers don't do hiding in bushes, especially on dark, damp evenings. It's a large, traditional thatched cottage, of a type and in a location highly sought after as a weekend retreat for investment bankers and hedge fund managers, which means it must have been inherited or married into, because the owner is Jim Bradman, the new Treasury minister, and there's no way a career politician like Jim could have earned enough to buy it himself by the age of thirty-eight.

Crouching beside me in the darkness is Happy Mboku, identifiable in the darkness only by his eyes and the gleam of his teeth. And next to him the large, lumpy mass is Nob, and next to him Sly and Timur and the rest of the team, and yes, we're wearing black – in my case Ralph Lauren chinos and a full-length highwayman's jacket with hood by Necessary Evil. I'm too old to go Gothic. I got through the whole of the internet boom and the new media bubble without ever going black, but here I am now, forced to wear something that, in some circles would be considered cool, but which senior investment bankers would sneer at. And all so I can sneak around in the darkness and not get spotted. Goodbye dignity, bring on expediency. This had better work.

What I'm hoping to do is talk to Bradman. And I mean really talk – the kind that politicians rarely do, because I'll need him to be listening, rather than in transmit mode. I'm taking a huge risk, but there aren't many alternatives and I'm calculating that there's just a chance that someone naive and idealistic enough to devote their political life to the Lib Dems will listen to what I have to say, think about it and do something, using his position in government to rein in the bad guys. Which bad guys? All of us. The bad guys and the worse guys. MI5, Bang Bang and Rom, even me. We need to bring this whole show under control. Do I have a shot? We'll see. All I know is the odds have to be better than trying to hide for the rest of my life with one of the most beautiful, desirable, noticeable women in the world on my arm. Fat chance of that working.

We saw him arrive, alone, about half an hour ago. No detective, no wife, no kids. What we don't know is whether anyone else is going to show up any time soon. It's a Thursday night and he's come to the country to spend Friday doing constituency business, because Parliament won't be sitting. For all I know he's come here for an evening of drug-crazed debauchery with his mistress/boyfriend/Alsatian, or the whole of the local Women's Institute.

I get up and slip and slide over the lawn, pick my way over the flowerbeds and creep round to the front door, staying low as I pass the windows.

The front door is locked, but Sly is right behind me and it takes him less than ten seconds with a set of lock picks to open up, stand back and wave me in.

Bizarrely, I'm conscious of my muddy feet on the carpet. Why do I think of something like this now? God knows. I can hear classical music coming from the living room and creep forward on my hands and knees. When I get to the living room door, I peer round it slowly. Bradman's sitting in an armchair, reading a book, with what looks like a glass of whisky beside him. He's peaceful, relaxed, nicely self-contained and, above all, looks mature. He's the kind of man I'd be in the evenings if I wasn't snorting coke and shagging hookers. He's at ease with himself. Part of me is disappointed that I haven't found him on his hands and knees in women's clothing, being whipped by a dominatrix.

I suppose that's what comes of allowing the Lib Dems into politics. And part of me is deeply jealous that he can be so self-contained, and look so wise and content when no one's watching and he doesn't need to pretend.

And then I lean too hard on the door and it creaks and swings open. Bradman's eyes go wide as he sees me lying on his living room carpet, watching him.

'Hart – what the hell are you doing here?' Bradman yells the words and turns to one side, presumably looking for some kind of panic button. That's when he notices the row of faces staring in at us at the window, starting with Happy Mboku's.

'Christ almighty. Who are these people?' He leaps to his feet and looks around, and I'm afraid he's searching for a weapon. I need to take charge of the situation.

I get to my feet, put my arms out to show I'm unarmed and, in my smarmiest, most oleaginous voice, oozing what I hope is reassurance, start to explain.

'Minister – I just want to talk to you. And these are my associates. We all want to talk to you.'

He stops panicking for a moment, stares back at the faces at the window, looks at me, takes a deep breath and is just about to try to calm down and work out what's going on, when Sly peers round the door behind me, complete with jagged scar and eye patch. Bradman turns and bolts for the other door.

It looks as if it leads to the kitchen, and I dash forward to cut him off, slamming my weight against it and standing there, panting, not sure which of us is more afraid.

'Minister, please. There's something we need to talk about.' I'm struggling to get my breath back, which is probably a good thing, because he can see how harmless and ineffectual I am. 'Minister, there's something going on that you need to know about, involving organised crime, the secret service and some very unpleasant people. There's an awful lot at stake here. Many tens of billions of pounds. Jobs and investments. The reputation of the City of London. And a once-in-a-lifetime chance to get some of the biggest criminal organisations in the world to go straight. The drugs trade could be halved overnight, human traffickers put out of business, racketeering brought to an end – because the bad guys are let inside the tent on condition they go clean. This is huge, and we need to talk about it. Now, tonight, because time is short. And it needs a decisive political intervention by someone who understands risk, who isn't afraid. A real man. This could be your big moment. The moment that decides where you go in politics . . . and in life.'

SO WHAT do you think he did? He's a Lib Dem, for fuck's sake. These guys yearn to play a part. They'll jump into bed with anyone if there's a chance of power and glory, and they'd sell their grandmothers for a place in the history books. Just look at the coalition. People think the Lib Dems are innocents abroad when it comes to realpolitik. The truth is, because they've been out of power for generations, giving them access to the kind of toy box politicians get to play with is like giving whisky and car keys to seventeen-year-old boys. Or, as I've said before, like putting someone like me in charge of a major financial institution.

We talked for hours. Happy and the guys came in and cooked us supper. So I explained all about the Salvation Fund, our investments, our plans and our backers. And the deal we'd made with them if we delivered. I told him about the goons in the office, HMG's heavy breathers, who could fuck everything up if they were allowed to. And I went to great lengths to explain that an opportunity like this wouldn't come along more than once in a lifetime. If he played it right, it could be transformational. It would need the prime minister's intervention, it would need the heavy breathers called off, it would need an amnesty – probably a secret one – for some serious heavy hitters who made their names hitting people. And the upside? The kind of one-off financial boost for the UK that the Bundesbank and the Fed could only dream about, the chance to tackle crime in a way that no other generation in history had been offered, and a fairy tale ending for me, where I get the girl and live to enjoy her.

Oh, and then there's the billion. The 'quiet billion' that only he and I would ever know about. The private part, a kind of special reserve that he could use for good causes. Any good causes he chose. The prime minister could have one too if he wanted. And the chancellor. In fact there'd be enough for everyone to have one if they wanted. At least all the people who count at times like this.

At first he didn't believe me. You wouldn't, would you? But as a politician he could tell a lie when he heard one, and after a while he worked out that he wasn't hearing any. When it was clear that he got it and wanted to grab it, I called Two Livers and she joined us for the final briefing session to prep him for the big call.

And around 6 a.m., when we'd run through it enough times and judged that he was ready, he called the prime minister and woke him up.

EPILOGUE

So I got my nest. Well, sort of.

I'm sitting on a bench in St James's Park, looking at the ducks on the water. I do this occasionally when I want to get my thoughts together. I think I've achieved a kind of stability. And I think I've found happiness too, or at any rate a version of it that works for me. Happiness is not waiting for anything new to happen. I've only had sex with one woman in the past year. A lot of times, admittedly, but I haven't strayed. She's amazing. She keeps surprising me. I'm besotted with her and so far I've been utterly, uncompromisingly faithful. Well, mostly.

I do very few drugs these days, just a few lines of coke and a little weed, because I find I don't need them as much, and I haven't been pissed in months. At least, not really pissed. I have a nightly martini when I'm in London, and most days I have a cigar, and a bottle of wine with dinner, and a nightcap, and I still drink at lunchtimes, and I really go for it on a Friday, but Fridays have always been different. Most of the time I'm off the booze because I'm finding stimulation elsewhere.

I'm smartly dressed. Today is a special day. And beside me the woman I love looks like a billion dollars. Or maybe ten billion. She's wearing a formal Burberry trench coat buttoned up to the neck, with a pashmina. I can't actually see if she's wearing anything else underneath. There are times when she doesn't, when she wants to surprise me. But today I know she is, because we're going somewhere special.

We're going to a celebration at the House of Lords. It's the second anniversary of that extraordinary day when I was forced to come clean about the Salvation Fund to a politician.

Jim Bradman didn't believe it at first, but once he got it he really went for it. Stuff like this doesn't fall into your lap every day of the week. And he took it to the top, explaining the risks, talking them through where it all might lead, passionately advocating the importance of allowing people – even wicked people – to change. We'd done it in different conflicts around the world, so why not use the same techniques in the conflicts that make our streets such dangerous places? Draw a line and allow people to come in from the cold. Bringing their money with them, of course.

And they did.

They had to do it secretly, and so the Salvation Fund continued until Grossbank bought it out and the investors got their money back. The team retired rich and happy, and I still see them from time to time. Maria got her million, and so did Tom.

And what did I get?

You know what I got.

I got the girl.

I turn and smile at her and she smiles back. Her fingernails are painted a very dark purple and she runs them along my thigh.

I want to wrap my arms around her, but I know I can't. Not now anyway. 'Later. We have to go now.'

We get up and walk to the road, where Tom is waiting in an immaculate black Rolls Royce Phantom. His, not mine. It was his birthday last week and I thought he deserved it.

'House of Lords, Tom, peers' entrance.'

We drive along Birdcage Walk towards the Palace of Westminster, passing the Treasury as we go. When we swing into the Lords, I hear Tom say to the policeman on duty, 'Sir David and Lady Hart, to see Lord Lee and Lord Romanov.'

Well, I had to make an honest woman of her, didn't I? A monstrous diamond and sapphire ring gleams on her finger beside a small gold band. The diamond was a gift from Rom, who insisted he had acquired it legitimately from the people of Sierra Leone and it was the least he could do after all the billions I made him. And the small bulge on her front isn't the start of a martini gut. I'm going to be a father again, and Two Livers is almost dry these days while she carries our son inside her. Imagine that. A young Dave Hart. I wonder what he'll be like. I guess that's for the nanny to find out.

I suppose that will be part of the next chapter. I'm desperately conscious that we need to grow together as a couple. Otherwise life will get boring again, and the devil makes work for idle hands.

We get out of the car and there are Bang Bang and Rom, waiting to take us in to a special celebration lunch. The chancellor, Jim Bradman, will be there, and Carlos, who has an honorary knighthood, and Bang Bang's bringing half the cast of *Kill Bill*, and no doubt Rom will have some of the undead there too, and there'll be a bunch of other familiar faces. Happy runs his own security firm now, and Nob is opening a sumo school. We're all starting new chapters in our lives. They're even tipping Jim Bradman as the next prime minister. Now that's interesting. Imagine what we could do if we ran the country . . . I shelve the thought. For now, anyway. Though I like to think big.

Dan Harriman isn't here. He's eight thousand miles away. The Foreign Office runs open competitions now for senior posts overseas, and Dan's got a new job as governor of the Falkland Islands. Apparently it's quite nippy this time of year, and there's a shortage of attractive young women. Last I heard the sheep were looking worried. But it was better than Bang Bang's alternative.

I look around the entrance hall. Once upon a time this place used to be full of crooks and brigands and robber barons. Has it really changed now? Of course not. It's just back to the future. Some bad guys can turn out to be surprisingly good, and when they're not good, at least they're interesting.

We go into the cloakroom to hang our coats, and mine is taken by a pretty Asian girl in a black uniform skirt and a white blouse, with dark eyes and long black hair. She's wearing perfume – not too much, just enough – and I can't quite place it. I look at her and she catches my eye and smiles. She has perfect white teeth and a mischievous dimple in her cheek. She keeps smiling as I look her up and down and wonder what lingerie she's wearing underneath her uniform. What to do? I know what I have to do. I'm happily married now, with a wedding band on my finger, and I'm not going to stray. I've changed. I'm not a player anymore. The past is the past.

On the other hand, a year is a long time to be married. I smile back at her and look her in the eye . . .